Murder
Most Familiar

MARJORIE BREMNER

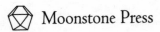 Moonstone Press

This edition published in 2022 by Moonstone Press

www.moonstonepress.co.uk

Introduction © 2022 Moonstone Press

Originally published in 1953 by Hodder & Stoughton, London

Murder Most Familiar © 1953 The Estate of Marjorie Bremner

The right of Marjorie Bremner to be identified as author of this work has been
asserted in accordance with the Copyright, Designs and Patents Act 1988

ISBN 978-1-899000-48-7
eISBN 978-1-899000-49-4

A CIP catalogue record for this book is available from the British Library

Text designed and typeset by Tetragon, London
Cover illustration by Jason Anscomb
Printed and bound by CPI Group (UK) Ltd, Croydon, CRO 4YY

Contents

Introduction

It is always a special treat to come across a novel that is both a fantastic read and virtually unknown to modern audiences. Such a story is *Murder Most Familiar*, first published by Hodder & Stoughton in 1953. Initially, the setting seems like relatively standard fare for English crime fiction: a country house, a murder, the family as suspects. What sets the book apart are the political overtones (covering a range from Communism to Fascism) and the sure touch author Marjorie Bremner brings to her characters. Told from the perspective of niece–secretary Christina, the challenges of dealing with a tough political tycoon in the family are evident from the first sentence: "My Uncle Hugh was the kind of man it was very easy to hate, if you were not susceptible to his particular kind of charm." The "uneasy relations between relations" and the ensuing internecine conflicts make Inspector Burgess' job all the harder. In their monumental compendium *A Catalogue of Crime* (1971), reviewers Jacques Barzun and Wendell Hertig Taylor described *Murder Most Familiar* as "top-notch", "subtly done" and "extraordinarily adroit".

Marjorie Bremner was born on 13 June 1916 in Chicago, the daughter of Ukrainian immigrants. Her father was a dentist and education was clearly valued: she received a BA in psychology from the University of Chicago, and a master's from Columbia University. Bremner worked as a psychologist in the women's branch of the United States Naval Reserve (known as the WAVES) during the Second World War and went to London in 1946 to work on a PhD in political science. She became a researcher for the Hansard Society, published articles on social and political problems, reviewed books and wrote the occasional light-hearted article in the newspapers (such as a tongue-in-cheek piece from 1956 that discussed the merits of encouraging children to watch TV as punishment).

Bremner's background in psychology, societal issues and politics came together in *Murder Most Familiar*, where the hidden tensions in a political family and the growth of a neo-fascist party are very well drawn. The novel garnered good reviews and a second, *Murder amid Proofs*, followed in 1955, but after these brief adventures in crime, Bremner returned to social and political commentary. In 1959, she married economist David Graham Hutton, and became his partner in work, a vivacious hostess to his wide international network, and stepmother to his three daughters. Bremner's retirement from the publishing world was sufficiently complete that by 1977 Hodder & Stoughton were forced to place an advert in the (London) *Times* asking for information regarding her whereabouts.

Without giving away any secrets, the cause of death in *Murder Most Familiar* is eventually explained in some clinical detail. For interested readers, a Google (Scholar) search will reveal a pharmacological review article that traces the history of the substance in question … and in it a reference to Marjorie Bremner!

Murder
Most Familiar

MY FAMILY

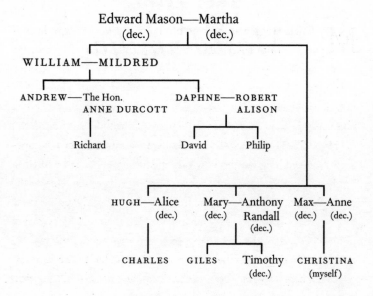

Edward Mason—Martha
(dec.)   (dec.)

WILLIAM——MILDRED

ANDREW—The Hon.   DAPHNE—ROBERT
ANNE DURCOTT   ALISON

Richard   David   Philip

HUGH—Alice   Mary—Anthony   Max—Anne
(dec.) (dec.)   Randall   (dec.) (dec.)
(dec.)

CHARLES   GILES Timothy   CHRISTINA
(dec.)   (myself)

I

My Uncle Hugh was the kind of man it was very easy to hate, if you were not susceptible to his particular kind of charm. He had of necessity hurt a lot of people on his way up, and he had learned to be tough. Perhaps he always had been and had no need to learn. A man does not leave school at fourteen, make a fortune by forty, and go on to become a skilful and powerful politician without ruthlessness.

My Uncle Hugh's career, besides demonstrating his own competence, showed how far and how fast an entire family can be lifted in England in only one generation, by the efforts of one man. He was the second of four children. He came from a working-class home. None of his brothers or sisters—not William, nor Hugh himself, Mary, or my father, Max—stayed in school beyond their fourteenth birthday. No member of my family, before my own generation, had ever been well-educated, kept a servant, been to the Continent, or been in a position to waste money or to indulge in luxurious tastes.

The photographs in our family album to-day tell a very different story. There are innumerable groups taken at Uncle Hugh's estate, Feathers. (From the album it could be assumed we spent a disproportionate amount of our time having tea in the garden.) There are pictures of the boys at Eton; of Daphne at school; of myself at school and at Newnham. We appear skiing, sailing, riding, and playing tennis. There is an elaborate photograph of Daphne's wedding at St. Margaret's, Westminster; a snap of Charles, elegant and amused, as best man at Andrew's wedding to the Honourable Anne Durcott. And all this—the transition from the working class to Feathers and everything that went with it—was done by just one man. It was perhaps not the least part of his achievement.

It is, of course, education that can transplant an entire family from one class to another far higher in the social scale so quickly and with so little pain. Uncle Hugh's task would have been much harder, though, had it been necessary for him to take a large number of adult relatives with him—or even his own wife. But she died in the third year of their marriage, leaving an only son, Charles.

Uncle Hugh had two brothers and one sister. My father, Max, was his younger brother. He and my mother were killed when I was five, and Uncle Hugh took over my guardianship. The only girl of the family, Mary, married a man called Randall, had one son, Giles, and died giving birth to her second son, Timothy. Her husband succumbed to an old war wound a matter of months later, and my uncle assumed care of the two boys as well. So the only adults he took with him on his climb were his older brother, William, and William's wife, Mildred. The couple had two children, Andrew and Daphne.

My Uncle William had none of his brother's ability. Nor did he have his charm, though he could on occasion produce a sort of bonhomie which passed for personableness with the less critical. He developed a certain competence in the narrow field of accounting, though he was never able to think of finance or of economics in broad, general terms. He may have been of a certain amount of use to Uncle Hugh, and he was naturally devoted to his brother's interests since his own were inseparable from them. But I do not believe Uncle Hugh relied on his brother's judgment in any serious or complicated matters, and though he continued to give William more money and more prestige, William was never really important in the business.

My Uncle William was not a fool. I doubt whether he dwelt much, deliberately, on the differences between his brother and himself. But unconsciously—and sometimes even consciously—he must have been aware of them; and they must have rankled. I never heard him anything but polite to Uncle Hugh. But sometimes when only we children were about, he allowed himself the luxury of a sly dig or a piece of corrosive wit. I don't know whether I really understood these barbed remarks at the time, or whether I only came to understand what Uncle William had meant as I grew up. Nor do I know whether Uncle Hugh was aware of his brother's deep resentment and jealousy. Uncle Hugh was a man of considerable reserve, and I seldom knew what he was thinking, still less what he felt.

My knowledge of my Uncle Hugh's deeper thoughts and feelings was not measurably increased by the years I spent with him as his personal assistant on the political side. (A man called George Tay had for years been his personal assistant in the business, a position which my Uncle William's son, Andrew, had strong ambitions to fill.) These years began shortly after the war ended. My job, which had been interesting and exacting, finished with the war, and I had no idea what I wanted to do next. My Cambridge ambitions had disappeared in the wake of a brief (and unwise) marriage and the responsible job at which I had overworked for nearly three years. I had read political economy and history at Cambridge, and had always been interested in politics, so that on those grounds it was perhaps reasonable for my uncle to offer me the job. It was characteristic of him to do so though he knew I did not share his political beliefs; and characteristic of me, no doubt, that I took the path of least resistance—and the job.

Working with my uncle, I began to appreciate his great energy and his ability; and I came to understand the reasons for his success. It was not due to outstanding intellectual ability. He was intelligent, but I have met many men more able in that way. For sheer intellectual ability, both his son Charles and our cousin Giles surpassed him, and Andrew was probably his equal. Nor, though he had a good deal of rather blunt, personal charm, was it primarily due to personal magnetism. But he had, coupled with energy and a clear mind, an undeviating steadiness and strength of will; good judgment and a good sense of timing; unimpaired self-confidence; the hide of a rhinoceros; and very few scruples. With that equipment, it would have been much more surprising if he had *not* been successful.

Working with my uncle proved over the years to be steadily and increasingly interesting. But it was demanding and wearing, and I welcomed the respites which sometimes came when Uncle Hugh decided to take one of his trips to the provinces without me. So I was not especially pleased when a last-minute change of plan, one Monday in the spring of 1952, made it necessary for me to accompany him to Birmingham at barely an hour's notice.

Raikes, the chauffeur, who had been with us for about fifteen years, was driving. My uncle and I sat in the back, composing a speech which enthusiastically ascribed all our current difficulties to the past follies of the Labour governments. How much my uncle believed of what we were writing I am not sure: perhaps half, more probably less. But it was developing into an amusing speech and I hoped we would finish it before our first stop at Oxford, where my uncle had some affairs to attend to.

But we did not finish the speech. We were about ten miles from Oxford, doing sixty-five miles an hour on the main road, when the front tyre exploded with a roar. Raikes did the best he could, but the combination of speed and the heavy car were too much for him, and we left the road and turned over before coming to a stop in the ditch. It was a nasty smash, and a very lucky thing we were not all killed.

In fact, we got off very lightly. We all had cuts and bruises, and I had sprained my left wrist. That was all. The Automobile Association arranged for us to be taken to Oxford. Uncle Hugh there decided to continue his journey by train and to send Raikes back to London with me, in a hired car. Raikes arranged to meet him in Birmingham with one of our other cars, two days later.

I sat in front with Raikes on the way back. He was an extremely good chauffeur and he had taken great pride in the Daimler, which was fairly new. "I don't understand it, Miss Christy," he kept saying at intervals of about five miles. "Those tyres had just been checked. There was nothing wrong with them. There was no reason for that one to go. And there was nothing on the road I could see—no nails or glass—that could have caused it."

I shrugged my shoulders. "These things happen every day. Don't worry about it, Raikes. My uncle doesn't blame you. Anyone can blow a tyre."

Raikes looked unconvinced. He had never had an accident before, and I think he considered a flat tyre a slur on his professional integrity. I did not feel well enough to argue about it with him.

News of the accident naturally made all the papers. "Millionaire Escapes Death", "Industrialist's Niece Hurt in Car Smash", "Ex-Cabinet Minister Speaks in Spite of Crash", and so on. Luckily, there was not much of a story, and a railway accident drove us out of the headlines very quickly.

The family, however, was more of a nuisance. Our own doctor came in as soon as I got back to London and insisted that I go to bed for a few days. "Your recent trip to America doesn't seem to have been much of a rest," he remarked. "You still need one. And shock is shock."

"Uncle Hugh's been shocked, too," I pointed out. "Why not try putting him to bed?"

"Partly because he wouldn't go. But even though he's sixty and you're only half his age, you need it more. He's got tough nerves. You haven't. You know, there's no point in over-estimating your endurance, Christy. I've been thinking of pointing that out to you for some time."

I made some evasive answer, but he was not put off. "Things affect you more than they do him. And—even though you won't talk about it—you've got something on your mind. Too many things, from the look of you."

"I'm terrified that Labour will win the next election," I said. "I'm equally terrified that the Conservatives will. It's enough to worry anyone."

"All right," said the doctor, getting up. "You're as bull-headed as your uncle, even if you haven't got his nerves. But you stay in bed several days anyway."

My being in bed naturally put me at the mercy of my family. I must except from this my cousin Giles, who having become a violent Left-wing Socialist in his Cambridge days, had more or less severed general social contacts with his family, though he did meet some of us from time to time.

But the others came to see me, singly and in pairs. They sent flowers, they rang up, and my cousin Charles even telephoned from the Embassy in Paris, where he was then stationed. After more or less perfunctory inquiries about my health and Uncle Hugh's, they embarked with varying degrees of subtlety on matters of general family concern—chiefly the rivalry between my cousin Andrew and Tay, and how it was progressing. My family's attentions probably retarded my recovery by a day or two.

If my family's attentions contributed something to the general sense of strain I was feeling, a conversation I had with Raikes on his return contributed much more. He came in to see me as soon as he returned with my uncle. Apparently satisfied with my condition, he plunged directly into the subject of the accident. His first remark was unpromising. "That was no accident, Miss Christy. I'm sure of it."

It was evident that Raikes had more than a reasonable share of that estimable virtue, professional pride. I knew it would be unwise to enter into a discussion, but I could see no alternative. "What makes you think so?" I asked.

"Miss Christy, you know enough about cars to know that tyres—good tyres—don't blow out like that very often. Not for no reason, they don't. And there was no reason—no glass, no nails."

We had been over all that *ad nauseam*. I did not say so. "It could have been an inferior tyre," I suggested.

"It wasn't, Miss Christy. I'm sure of that. And I didn't like that accident. I didn't like it at all. Why, if someone had wanted to kill your uncle, he couldn't have found a better way to do it."

"If someone—Raikes, you can't be serious!"

"Hear me out, Miss Christy. Like I said, I didn't like it. It shouldn't have happened. And I got to thinking. If I wanted to wreck a car—and not show any traces of what I'd done—do you know the best way, Miss Christy?"

I shook my head.

"Well, you know, if you put too much pressure in a tyre—pump too much air in it—and then the tyre goes, there's no earthly way of telling what's been done. If I wanted to wreck a car, that's what I'd do."

"It sounds plausible," I said. "What doesn't sound plausible is that anyone should have tried to do it to my uncle's car. Have you any reason for thinking anyone wanted to?"

He did not answer directly. He said, "You know, Miss Chris, some people have the idea that I'm a bit fussy about where things are kept—maybe a little too neat, even."

This was a masterpiece of understatement. Raikes was the most meticulous man I have ever met. The garage was a model of order. There was seldom so much as a nail out of place. His clashes with careless members of the staff, in the London house and at Feathers, who had rashly moved some tool half a centimetre from its appointed place, were frequent and violent.

I agreed that I had heard some mention of his liking for order.

"Yes," said Raikes. "That's right, Miss Christy. Well, I've got a tyre pump in the garage. It has its place, same as everything else. The car wasn't out of the garage that Sunday before we left for Birmingham, and I checked it over just after tea—about five o'clock that afternoon. Checked the tyres, too—*and* saw everything was where it belonged. That tyre pump was in its place. I locked the garage when I took the car out the next morning. Well, when I came back from Birmingham,

I had a look for that pump. It was way over on the other side of the garage—away from its proper place."

He paused. I said, "I don't see what that proves. Anyone could have got in the garage. There's a spare key in the kitchen."

"I've asked the staff," said Raikes, doggedly. "They all say they didn't go near the place. Why should they, Miss Christy? None of them has a car or a bike—what would they do with a tyre pump?"

He did not mention that most of them, terrified of his fierce tidiness, would have taken very good care to have replaced the pump, had they borrowed it for any purpose. I sighed. "There are probably half a dozen reasonable explanations of how it came to be moved," I said. "All of them harmless."

Raikes did not answer. He looked stubborn—and unconvinced. I said, "Have you mentioned this to Sir Hugh?"

He shook his head. "Only to you, Miss Chris. Maybe you're right—it's only an idea. But I don't think so. And I thought—if anyone's trying to harm Sir Hugh—well, you're with him a lot when I'm not. You could sort of keep an eye on him."

The idea of myself as my uncle's bodyguard almost made me smile. I said, "You haven't said why you think anyone should want to harm my uncle—or whom you have in mind."

But this challenge Raikes would not take up. He just said he would keep a careful eye out, and he seemed to assume that I would do the same. Then he left. He had had, after all, no need to take up my challenge, and he knew it as well as I did. For that Sunday night, we had had a family dinner—the first in some months. Charles had been over for the week-end from Paris and Tay had come in to coffee. There had, I suppose, been ample opportunity for anyone to tamper with the tyre, if anyone had wanted to do so.

I don't know how a normally effective person would have reacted to Raikes' fears and suspicions, or how I myself would have reacted had the episode taken place while I was still at Cambridge, before I met

Simon. I think that at that time I might have been able to cope with it fairly well. But my brief marriage with Simon had paralysed my ability to deal easily with such things.

I had probably always been a little more reserved and detached than most English girls. Our family life, I think, was rather dry. Uncle Hugh was not an emotional man; he would not have chosen nurses or governesses who were. I had been, throughout my life, very clever at school, well-adjusted, friendly, and sociable, but somewhat remote all the same. Perhaps that was why passion, when it first touched me, shattered me so completely. I could never really make the bridge between myself as I had been and myself as I was after I met Simon. There were two halves, and I never put them together.

If a Cambridge degree has any value, it was fortunate that I did not meet Simon until the week after I had taken my exams—very successfully, as it turned out. I met him at a party on Saturday, and spent Sunday with him on the river. He was in the Navy, commanding one of those small patrol boats which took such frightening risks almost every night along the shores of Britain. He was admirably suited to it. I think the only reason he had not joined the RAF was that it seemed to him such a conventional form of danger—and of heroism.

The worst of it was that my judgment did not forsake me. I could have excused myself or come to terms with myself better if it had. If I had thought him other than what he was—better, kinder, more scrupulous, less of a sensationalist—I think I could have forgiven myself. One has to be much more arrogant than I was to believe one can never be wrong. But I was not mistaken in him. I saw him almost from the beginning, very, very clearly. I knew just what he was. I knew it would be unwise to see him, folly to love him, insane to marry him. But I could not help myself. I literally could not have refused anything he asked me. I never did. I was never free of him for a single moment from the first moment we met. When we were together with other people, I saw them through a kind of haze. He was the only real thing.

Why he married me, I never knew. It was not with any idea of a life-long union or steadfast faithfulness. Such ideas never crossed Simon's mind. The only thing that did cross his mind was the life of the present—excitement, danger, sensation; and nothing else. He was killed eighteen months after our marriage. During those eighteen months, I lived on an emotional plane that I would never willingly live on again. I literally never thought of anything but him. Even when I was doing something I liked, talking to other people, seeing a play, he was never very far below the surface of my consciousness: where was he, what was he doing, was he thinking of me? It was an obsession and I knew it; but I could do nothing about it.

We had a flat in London, and I did some war work. I wanted to take a regular job, but Simon would not hear of it. He wanted me there, at his disposal, when it pleased him to be with me. Of course I did as he wanted. He could generally be in London two or three times a week, but that did not mean, except in the first weeks of our marriage, that he spent his time with me. He spent it as he pleased—with me or with anyone or anything else that caught his fancy. Sometimes— very rarely—on a night when I did not expect him, I made another engagement. If he happened to come into London and found me planning to go somewhere, he sometimes insisted that I break whatever engagement I had made. I always wanted to do it. But sometimes, out of perversity and unkindness mixed, he would insist that I go, saying that he could easily amuse himself. I would rush through my evening and come home very early—usually before ten—even though I knew he would certainly not be in before midnight and would most probably not come home at all. And sometimes, unexpectedly, I would meet him at a party. I would see him across the room, a drink in his hand, smiling, his head bent a little forward to hear what the girl—he was always with a pretty girl—was saying; and I would feel my heart turn over.

I was not surprised when he was killed. I knew the chances he took, and it was a wonder he lasted as long as he did. I was just stunned—too stunned even to feel a very sharp grief or the relief of knowing that I could now belong to myself once more. I went through the normal movements of living, but it was all a blur at the time. It remained a blur. I could never say with accuracy what I did, what I said, or how I spent my time, in the weeks immediately following his death. A few months later, while still in a daze, I was offered a job at one of the Ministries. I accepted; and there I spent the rest of the war.

I gradually came to appear more like my normal self. But this did not come about because I was able to accept what had happened to me with Simon and to integrate it with the rest of myself. Instead, I repressed my memories of Simon and the emotions that went with him fiercely, almost savagely. As a result, the memory, instead of mellowing, festered. Many years later, I still winced when I heard his name, or slept badly for nights if someone spoke of him to me.

But that was not all. I could not accept what had happened to me because I could not trust myself any more. I had walked into an emotionally damaging situation, knowing it for what it was, and unable to stop myself. For the most part, I could repress the memories of it, or at least the most painful ones. I could not repress—or forgive—the knowledge of my own weakness. I no longer felt able to act freely in any situation in which my own emotions were involved. I could act efficiently and make decisions which concerned my work. But I could not deal with my own life with confidence. At any hint of an emotional situation, I froze—and then escaped.

That was why, when my uncle offered me a job after the war and suggested that I come back to live in his house, I accepted. I rationalized to myself that it was a very interesting job—which it was; and that I would be very comfortable—which I was. What I did not admit consciously was that with my Uncle Hugh, I was safe. He would make no demands on me I could not meet without strain; and there would be no difficult decisions for me to take. Uncle Hugh would cope with them, too. But unconsciously I must have known all this; and it must have been the real reason I took the job.

Some people are able, in circumstances like this, to fall back on the support and the affection of their family—or at least of some members of it. But I couldn't. Uncle Hugh had helped me, certainly, but not consciously, and not with my real problem. No other member of my family could do anything at all; and the idea of my united family as a source of collective support never entered my head. It would have been a most unrewarding idea. We had always been a rather uneasy family, and the stresses and strains and rivalries among us were numerous and deep.

Numerous—there was always a strain between my Uncle William and my Uncle Hugh (I put it that way since my Uncle Hugh was in no sense disturbed by the relationship). My Aunt Mildred was uneasy with all of us—wildly ambitious for her husband and children, determined (as was her husband) that Andrew should succeed to my Uncle Hugh's position, and jealous that Charles, Giles, Timothy, and I had been brought up in Uncle Hugh's house; though since Charles was Uncle Hugh's only son, it is difficult to understand where else she would have thought it suitable for him to have been raised. Giles had long been bitterly at odds with Uncle Hugh and somewhat less bitterly at odds with the rest of us. Charles was ironically detached and inclined to bait his relations, especially Andrew and—when he saw him—Giles. Andrew—Daphne—the catalogue could go on at length.

Of course, many families are like this. Few can boast of smooth relations between all their members. But various factors combined to make ours worse, or at least more complicated, than most. Our family had come up very quickly. Perhaps because of that, perhaps for other reasons, most of us were cool rather than naturally warm-hearted. We were all more than normally self-willed. And we all, in a way, revolved about or were dependent upon, the arrogant and powerful figure of my Uncle Hugh.

If, in view of our uneasy relations with each other, we had been able to let each other alone, none of this would have mattered very much. But we could not.

It was not that we were especially intimate; on the contrary, we each seemed to be enclosed in our isolated selves. But any little action by any one of us seemed to be reported all round—reported and reacted to. We were not a large family, and we did not usually move in the same circles. But if two of us met and clashed at a dinner-party, as Giles and I had more than once done; if the rivalry between Tay and Andrew for the future control of my uncle's business reached new heights; if Charles got up to something in Paris; if anything, large or small, happened, the combination of a bush telegraph and a sixth sense seemed to ensure that everyone else in the family would sooner or later hear all about it. Some kind of vast *malaise* seemed to exist among us. The only person entirely unaffected by any currents or counter-currents was my Uncle Hugh.

The only person unaffected by family currents and cross-currents, yes; but in the past year, especially since our return from America, I had found my Uncle Hugh somewhat different. I had seen less of him than usual—he seemed to go off on his own more often. I learned on inquiry that he did not take Tay and Andrew with him any more than usual. I had made one or two rather guarded inquiries among my relatives, to see if anyone else had remarked this change in him. But I received looks so blank and suggestions so absurd (my Aunt Mildred thought he might be planning to marry again) that I gave it up. Eventually, I had become used to his new or slightly changed manner of behaving; but when I reviewed in my mind my feeling of discomfort about the family, the change in Uncle Hugh came back to me with force.

II

Confined to bed, worried by my family, and disturbed over Raikes' suggestions, I did not make a quick recovery. Nor, outside of unproductive worrying, did I take any action at all. Though my wrist healed rapidly, I continued to feel tired and disinclined to do anything.

How long this state of affairs might have lasted, I don't know. But fortunately, before it had gone on for more than a few days, my uncle had to go to a Conference. He did not actually need me, but I knew that I could be very useful to him if I went along. I did, and it turned out to be a very good idea. The Conference itself was surprisingly interesting, and my uncle helped to raise my morale by telling me I was looking very well. "Several of the men complimented me on your looks," he said, though he was not usually given to remarks of this kind. "I didn't point out that I could claim little credit for them. Of course, you know how to dress, and that always helps."

After the Conference, I fell back into my normal routine; and Raikes'—on reflection, rather melodramatic—remarks faded in my mind. In any case, I had a good deal else to think about. A fortnight after I had returned to work, Paul Meadows rang up and asked me to dine with him. Paul was a journalist, with Right-wing Labour sympathies. I had known him since Cambridge.

"Can you make it early?" he asked. "I'd like you to come with me to a meeting—the Freemen of Britain. Remember them?"

We had been to a meeting of the Freemen two or three years earlier. Paul had thought there might be a story in it. I had expected a variant of the many small, crank political groups that flourish in London, and had been somewhat surprised to find it more like an ordinary, small political meeting. The proceedings had started quarter of an hour late, with the National Anthem. The three speakers had been adequate but not outstanding. I was even then an old hand at political meetings, and I thought the chief fault at this one was that the speakers had tried to make too many points. The audience, however, had been courteous and attentive—it seemed largely lower-middle-class—and had stayed until the meeting had closed, at about 10.45, again with the National Anthem. Afterwards, I had remarked to Paul that it had all seemed rather an amateur affair. "I suppose your party's calling it semi-Fascist?"

Paul had looked puzzled. "I suppose so. Did you think it was Fascist?"

"I didn't think it was much of anything. I doubt whether the organizers—whoever they may be—know what they're driving at, outside of expressing a little discontent. For a while, when that second man—what was his name? Simpkins, wasn't it?—well, when Simpkins was speaking, I thought I caught a whiff of the old Disraeli-Randolph Churchill idea. Tory democracy. An alliance between the true leaders of the people and the masses. The new freedom. You know that sort of thing. But nothing came of it."

Paul had agreed with me, and we had dropped the subject. Since then, I suppose I had come across announcements of the Freemen of Britain from time to time, but I had never paid much attention to them.

I told Paul I remembered the Freemen of Britain. "I didn't find the meeting especially exciting," I said. "Have you some particular reason for going to-night?"

"Yes," said Paul. "I have. And I'd like you to come along. You'll be interested."

So we went for a second time to a meeting of the Freemen of Britain. It was so different that it was hard to believe it was the same organization. For one thing, the meeting was a fairly big one, held in a large hall. More important, it was clear that a professional touch had invaded the organization. I have seldom seen a meeting handled so well.

It began promptly at 8.15, as announced. It did not begin with the singing of the National Anthem. At precisely 8.15, three men and a woman walked on to the platform. The woman and one of the men were middle-aged. One of the men was older, and the third looked in his middle twenties. They were all well dressed, but not ostentatiously so, and looked solid, respectable, and intensely English. The old man looked like a judge. The middle-aged man was in the chair.

They were all excellent speakers: clear, simple, and precise. They did not confuse the audience with a host of unrelated points. They made few demands on the intellectual capacity of their listeners. They had a few points, and they each made the same ones, several times. But so cleverly were their speeches written that I don't suppose one person in ten realized that all the speakers had said the same things.

Each spoke for about twenty minutes. There were then a number of questions, well-asked and well-answered. The Chairman then read the Creed of the Freemen of Britain, and asked those who agreed with it to say "Aye". The audience responded "Aye", and sang the National Anthem. The four walked—almost marched—off the platform, and the meeting was over. It was then exactly 9.30.

I had been to meetings in Nazi Germany and in Italy, before the war. This was nothing like them. There were no uniforms, no chants like "*Sieg Heil*", no army of flags, no songs: just an ordinary hall in London, four average-looking English people, a short creed which no one had to repeat, and the National Anthem. Yet for no reason I could understand, I had something of the same chilled feeling I had had at those openly Fascist meetings. There was something menacing in the air. But I could not have put my finger on what it was.

Yet someone had caught the essence of the original and rather pathetic little organization whose meeting I had attended nearly two years earlier. The Freemen of Britain had had one point, then: a modern version of the old Tory Democracy of Disraeli and Randolph Churchill. It was not a version either of those two men would have accepted. But all the same, it could be effective. Disraeli had seen an organization of the working classes and the aristocracy. So did this Freemen of Britain, though it had widened its concept of aristocracy. But the idea had been changed somewhat: and its essence now, if I understood it, was precisely what it had been in Germany: the surrender of their judgment and their will, by the ordinary people, to the aristocrats (whether of blood, brains, or money) who would lead them through the maze of the modern and confusing world.

The organizers of the Freemen did not make the mistake many organizers before them had of confusing England with the Continent. This movement was entirely English. The loud shouting in unison, the flags, the frenzied cheering, the slightly comical Fuehrer—all that was out. The speakers had appealed to the English love of country, but in a decent, reserved, English way, not with loud and "foreign" ranting. They had been very, very clever. And I admit that I was a bit frightened.

When the meeting was over, Paul and I went out to have a drink. He ordered whisky, and swallowed half of his in one gulp. "Well," he said, "what do you think of our little organization? Changed, hasn't it?"

"Yes," I said. "It's become very efficient. It impresses me. I might even say it frightens me somewhat."

Paul agreed. "It frightens me, too. These people are avoiding all the natural pitfalls into which a Fascist movement—if I may use an outdated word—so easily stumbles in England. With things as they are—if economic conditions get worse—this kind of thing just might succeed. What do you think?"

"I don't know," I said. "I don't know. Maybe."

Paul spread out the leaflet of the Freemen on the table. Some of the names listed on it were familiar to one or to both of us; others we had never heard of. "Half of them may be dummies anyway," he said. "Or at least they may count for very little. It's much more likely that the real brains don't choose to list themselves. They've got some real brains thinking for them—and somehow I don't think anyone on this list is among the thinkers."

"Waiting to see how the organization goes before coming out in the open? I suppose so. But there are the usual Fleet Street rumours?"

Paul shrugged his shoulders. "For what they're worth. I don't think anyone has any reliable dope yet."

We had another drink, and Paul asked me if I'd seen Giles lately. I told him no. "Then you've not met his girlfriend?"

"No," I said. "Certainly not. I didn't even know he had one. He's never been much of a womanizer, you know. Who is she?"

"Someone called Bella something-or-other. I think she paints. I don't think she's actually a Communist, but she's played around on the fringes a bit. You know the type."

"I do," I said, unenthusiastically. "Pretty?"

"No. Striking, though—hair drawn back, no make-up except dark lipstick, generally intense look."

"I could have guessed," I said, gloomily. "I wonder if he'll marry her."

"Would your uncle mind if he did?"

"Uncle Hugh? I shouldn't think so. After all, he'd probably never meet her. In any case, he doesn't consider Giles' life any of his business."

"Giles considers your uncle's life *his* business."

"That's different," I said.

Paul grinned. "It's funny to hear them in the House."

It was, in a way; though funny was not precisely the word I would have used. My uncle was a reasonably good parliamentarian, though he never was what would have been called primarily a "House of Commons man". But I had often been in the gallery when he had made a brief, forceful speech to the House. His accent, its Northern tones still very evident, sounded odd, coming after the educated Southern English accents one usually heard from his side of the House. But people did listen to him, his own side with respect and the Labour benches with dislike and anger.

And I had heard Giles speak after him, as he occasionally did. Giles was a brilliant speaker, caustic, witty, and trenchant. On the public platform, he spoke like a demagogue. In the House, he modified his manner to suit its convention, and very successfully. Whereas Uncle Hugh was slow, solid, and immensely forceful, Giles was swift, ironic, and biting. But the true irony of the situation lay in the fact that Giles had always looked enough like Uncle Hugh to be his son, not just his nephew; he resembled Uncle Hugh much more than Charles did, and the older Giles grew, the stronger the resemblance became. When Giles finished lacing into the Conservatives, there were always excited cheers from his own side. But when he did this immediately following a speech from Uncle Hugh, I seemed to detect some uneasiness in the cheers. The Honourable Members were not always sure then whether they were witnessing an attack on privilege or just an old family feud. They entirely liked the one; but they did not like the other—at least, not on the floor of the House of Commons.

Giles' career was at that stage progressing very well, though he was not in the government. He was active as a free-lance journalist and broadcaster, and was making a great deal of money. His views were so far Left, his anti-Americanism so militant, his criticisms of the Soviet Union so tepid that the more politically naïve often mistook him for a Communist or at least a fellow-traveller. The trade-unionists appeared to regard him with a mixture of admiration and mistrust. I don't believe that he had much influence in the top circles of the Labour Party—at least, not in those circles which were running the Party. But he was adored by the more emotional constituency parties, by Fabians, and by the more volatile readers of the Left-wing weeklies. He was in great demand to speak at public meetings and at local parties, and he always gave an outstanding performance. I sometimes wondered whether both family life and life in the Labour Party wouldn't have been easier if my cousin had decided to go on the stage instead of into politics.

I suddenly remembered a conversation I had had with my cousin Charles some years back, in 1949, or thereabouts, and I smiled. Paul asked what I was laughing at. "I was just remembering a conversation I had with Charles. He lives in horror of the day Giles gets into the government. He says the doctrine that responsibility steadies people down and makes them more bearable is on the whole true, but that Giles is the greatest living exception to it. I told Charles I'd voted Labour in 1945, and that they'd done a lot of things I hadn't liked—but that as long as Giles wasn't in the government, I'd stay inclined to the view that Mr. Attlee had some judgment left."

"Mr. Attlee, perhaps," said Paul, a bit gloomily. "But what about the Welsh wonder?"

I said I didn't know. Paul said, "Well, it may not come to that. But—since we've talked so much about Giles, why don't you come along to hear him to-morrow night? I have to cover his meeting, and I'd like company."

"Unless Giles' views have changed considerably, I know everything he's going to say."

"So do I. But it's always interesting to see his effect on the crowd. Besides, maybe his girlfriend has mellowed him a bit."

So we went along together. I hadn't heard my cousin speak for some time, and I'd forgotten how eloquent he could be. The large hall was jammed, and people were standing in the back and along the sides. Giles had just launched a violent attack on the United States, and it was evident that the crowd agreed with everything he said. I could catch phrases and sentences through the applause and the roars of cheers and laughter: "... tell you this great country of ours shall not knuckle under to the money-changers and war-mongers of Wall Street ... the American standard of living is bought at our expense ... they are bringing pressure on us constantly to cut our food subsidies further so that you, my friends, will have to go without the basic foodstuffs ... and meanwhile, they subsidize *their own farmers*. Yes. I said subsidize. The American government artificially keeps up the prices of farm products. So we have to pay more for them. That means we have to manufacture and export more to pay for them. And that, my friends, is why we cannot have at home more of the products—the high-quality products—that our British workers produce. So we British workers—who saved the world in 1940—*we* subsidize the American standard of living. *We* help to support the richest country in the world. I tell you it will not do! It shall not do!"

His next words were lost to me because of a storm of cheers and applause. When I could next make out what he was saying, he had switched to the subject of the Soviet Union and Eastern Europe: "... do not condone all the Russians have done. Nor do I defend their system. But they have much to blame us for. If they do not trust us now, we bear a large share of the blame. If they were good enough to fight with in the war, they are good enough to trade with now ... we can get wheat and lumber and the other things we need from them ..." he shouted, while his audience stamped in approval. "We can take the lead in uniting the progressive forces of Europe *including Russia* in a sensible economic system which has the welfare of the working classes as its goal. We can leave the American capitalists drowning in their own wheat and machinery and television sets and refrigerators until they beg us—*beg us*—to buy from them. And then *we* shall call the tune—and there will be a Labour Government in Britain to call it..."

This time, the cheering was even louder and more prolonged. When I could hear again, Giles was talking about home affairs: "... we are asked to tighten our belts and do without things while the rich ride around the West End in new cars driven by chauffeurs ... we pay P.A.Y.E. while they ask to lower the taxes on high incomes ... *and* don't pay their taxes now ... tell you I would shoot any man who didn't pay his income tax in times of economic crisis and volunteer for the firing-squad myself..."

"Giles," I said to Paul, under cover of the applause, "made £5,000 last year."

"Well," said Paul, a little apologetically, "Attlee doesn't talk like that."

"No. But he doesn't stop Giles or his friends. He doesn't even disown them."

"There are wild-eyed Conservatives whom Churchill doesn't disown."

"Oh, I know. It's just that we happen to be listening to Giles at the moment. I wonder if he'll tell them about how he was exploited at Eton."

When the meeting was over, we went around to see Giles. He was immensely exhilarated and quite affable, and agreed to come out for a drink with us. There was no sign of Bella. In the club, he downed two drinks rather quickly and asked me how my relatives were. I told him everyone was all right, and would have sent love had they known I was going to see him that night.

Giles grinned. "I'm sure. Everything all set for the great man's birthday party?"

"Yes," I said. "Why don't you come, too—and bring your girl?"

"You're an incredible girl, Christy. Where do you get all your information? Uncle Hugh running an intelligence service?"

"You underestimate your own importance, Giles. All kinds of people are interested in your affairs. Where is she to-night, by the way? I hoped to meet her."

"Well, I never met Simon," said Giles, smoothly. He went on, almost without a pause. "What's that power-driven uncle of yours up to now?"

I sensed something in the question beyond his usual gibe. It might almost have been anxiety. "Running the business," I said. "Making lots of money. What did you expect him to be doing?"

"I wouldn't put anything past him. Maybe he's developing new interests. And Tay—maybe he's developing new interests, too. What does *he* think of the Freemen of Britain?"

It was very sudden. "Tay? I don't know. What do you think of them?"

"I think they're bloody dangerous," said Giles. He rose abruptly. "I have to be off. Thanks for the drinks." He hesitated for a moment, and then put his hand on my shoulder. "Sorry, Chris. Didn't mean to be unpleasant."

"Oh, neither did I." We smiled at each other a bit uncertainly. Then he said good-night to Paul and left.

After we had had another drink, Paul and I went for a drive. He said, tentatively, "Do you dislike him?"

"Giles? No. He irritates me, of course—you saw that to-night. But—oh, he's my cousin, I grew up with him. I don't dislike him. And if I did, it wouldn't be in the ordinary way. We're too close for that. I'm sorry we exposed you to our family bickering, though."

He said it didn't matter. "You're an odd family, though. Giles— well, other people from wealthy families have become Socialists without finding it necessary to hate all their relatives in the process. Was he always that way about your Uncle Hugh?"

I thought back—to Giles at prep school with the other boys, to trips abroad, to holidays at Feathers. "No," I said, slowly. "I don't think he was. He was always—he had a tendency to be dissatisfied with things. He was more critical—or more rebellious—than the rest of us—at least, on the surface. In a way, when he was young, he was very much impressed by Uncle Hugh. He gibed at his achievements and his importance, but he noticed them. My cousin Charles—that's Uncle Hugh's only son—never paid any attention to what his father did. At least, he acted as if he didn't."

"You're an odd family," said Paul, for the second time. "I've met Charles, you know. He always seemed to me to be playing a part. Didn't his father mind when he wouldn't come into the business?"

"Perhaps we are odd, at that. Do you know, I don't know. I work with my uncle, I see a good deal of him—and yet I have no idea at all what he thinks of Charles or of what Charles has done. My Uncle William, of course—who's a menace—is sure Uncle Hugh's very much disappointed in Charles and that he wishes his son were like

Andrew. On the surface, that may be a logical idea. But I'm not at all sure it's true. You can never tell what Uncle Hugh thinks of things."

Paul smiled. "I suppose you can be sure of what he thinks of Giles."

"Not even that. I'll tell you something—though of course it's only a guess. I've always thought that if my uncle could find some way of making sure any money he left Giles wouldn't go to help start a new left-wing weekly—or something like that—he'd leave him a reasonable amount. I don't even know that he hasn't done it, though I'd bet against it."

"You've no idea how he's left his money?"

"Not the slightest—*nor* how he's planning to leave control of the company." The mention of money brought back to my mind for a moment its relation to the family uneasiness. I had often wondered if money were the chief root of it: that is, concern over what Uncle Hugh was going to do with his fortune. In a way, that seemed absurd. For one thing, we all had quite adequate incomes, though no capital. For another, Uncle Hugh was barely sixty and in excellent health. The chances were that he would continue in full control of his own affairs for well over a decade, barring accidents. And yet——

I realized abruptly that I was talking about rather personal family matters to an outsider. "I seem to be very talkative to-night. All these family details must be very dull. I'm sorry."

"Well, I egged you on. I was interested, though strictly speaking, it's none of my business. It must have been seeing you and Giles together to-night—and seeing Giles up there on the platform looking so incredibly like your uncle. He looks like your uncle, Andrew behaves like your uncle, and Charles is Sir Hugh's son. It's an unusual situation."

"It is," I agreed. "However, there are some simpler members of my family—like Andrew's sister, Daphne. She married the only son of a City baronet, she has two children, and so far as I know, there's nothing complicated about her."

"Robert Alison, isn't it—the young Tory M.P.? Yes, I know them. At least, I've seen them about a bit. She's interested in writing, isn't she?"

"Daphne?" I laughed. "Not to the best of my knowledge."

"I've seen her at some Author's League lunches, I'm sure of it. I don't think I could be mistaken. She's very decorative. But then, so are you. Why a girl with looks like yours and red hair at that ever took to politics, I'll never know."

"You can't really say I've taken up politics," I said. "I only hover around the edges."

It was getting late, and Paul drove me home. Just before we parted, he said, "You almost winced when he mentioned your husband. Do you still mind so much?"

"I—it's not that. I just don't like talking about it."

"You don't really like talking about anything personal, do you? Do you realize this is the first even slightly personal conversation we've ever had?"

"Some day," I said, "I'll tell you all about my Aunt Mildred—and you'll be sorry."

III

A few days later, Uncle Hugh gave a dinner. It was, like many, an all-male affair, and I only came in later, when they were all having coffee. They were apparently in very good humour, and were talking about economic conditions in Britain—not surprisingly, since most of the guests had rather a large stake in the country.

"The point," my uncle was saying, as I came in, "may well be that we've reached the end of parliamentary democracy—the end of its usefulness as a system, I mean. We're now in with a small majority. I doubt whether we'll get in next time—and if we should, it would be by the narrowest of margins."

There were mild protests at this. One Conservative optimist, convinced that another two years of Conservative government would see a great improvement in conditions and a strong swing to his party as a result, prophesied a majority of a hundred seats at the next election. My uncle shook his head.

"So far as I can see, this country's set. Everyone's made up his mind—and very few will change. Look. You have a situation in which certain things ought to be done. But they're politically impossible. The sensible men in both parties realize it. People want—the mass of the people want—to work less and live better. Can't be done. And no government is going to be elected—not with a large majority, anyway—which truthfully says it can't be done. Look at us during the last election. We didn't say it—one of the reasons our stock's so low now. People thought we could perform miracles—at least, some of the more naïve who voted for us thought they'd really get red meat at every meal within a month after we took office. And certainly Labour's not going to take the austere line."

One of the other guests, Lord Ravan, agreed with my uncle. "What happens next?"

"When a system doesn't work," said my uncle, "it is eventually replaced by one which will. It can happen accidentally or by design. But it's got to happen."

"The Russians," said Lord Ravan, "have a different system. You're not turning into a Communist, Mason?"

There was a general laugh. "Not a Communist," said my uncle, when it had subsided. "In fact, I'm not turning into anything. I'm just giving the situation some thought."

When the guests had gone, my uncle and I stayed in the drawing-room for a few minutes, talking, and I saw him take a pill from a small bottle and swallow. I asked if he weren't feeling well.

"No, I'm all right, Christy. But I had a slight digestive upset in Birmingham—the hotel doctor couldn't make out exactly what it was, though it wasn't anything serious. Barker (our own doctor) changed my digestive pills when I told him about it—said possibly the other kind wasn't agreeing with me—not that I take them often."

I did not say anything. But that night, I did not sleep very well, and I spent the next days in a state of anxiety and indecision. Normally, of course, a simple remark by my uncle that he had changed his pills because of a digestive upset would not have warranted a second thought. But coupled with Raikes' concern over our accident, it warranted more than that.

The trouble was that, so far as I could see, all paths were marked "no entry". With some difficulty, I faced up to the problem. Raikes had hinted at the possibility that someone might be trying to kill my uncle. He had no way of proving it, nor had I. The police, should we go to them, would probably brush aside as fantasy such a suspicion based on nothing more than Raikes' conviction the tyre had been all right—plus a misplaced tyre pump! Because of my uncle's position, they would probably accord me a good deal of courtesy and attention, none the less. One of their questions was bound to be: has your uncle any enemies? Do you know anyone who would want to harm him?

I did not. And if they were to push their inquiry further and say, "Who had access to the garage key?", the only answer I could give was: anyone. Anyone—including all the members of my family and Tay, who had dined at the house the night before the accident. It was not the sort of thing I could see myself saying to a police inspector.

I tried, over that week-end, to put the matter out of my mind. To reassure myself that my ideas were the product of two over-active imaginations—Raikes' and my own—I telephoned to various members of my family, ostensibly for the dual purpose of finding out how they were and discussing arrangements for the family house-party which was being held at Feathers the next week-end to celebrate my uncle's sixtieth birthday. My real motive was to convince myself of the essential normality of my relatives and the absurdity of my suspicions.

I spoke to Charles in Paris. He said that he was touched by my solicitude, that Paris was very gay, and that he understood that Giles had picked up a most curious girlfriend who lived, of all places, in Redcot. (As Redcot was the next village to ours, in the country, my interest in this piece of information was, like his, very great.) He sounded exactly the same as usual: amusing, detached, a little brittle, and perhaps—underneath it all—a little tough. I called Daphne, heard in boring detail about the health of Robert and the children, and asked her if it were true that she was developing an interest in the literary life. I thought her answer sounded embarrassed and a little slow in coming, but in general she sounded quite as usual. I rang up Andrew's wife, Anne, and carefully avoided all questions pertaining to Tay and the business. I had a word with Tay about a new play which we had both seen. (Even in view of the exigent circumstances, I was not willing to hold an extra conversation with my Uncle William, still less with my Aunt Mildred.) When I had finished these calls,

I had received no reassurance at all. If anything, my uneasiness was deepened, for I had been struck—as always—by the curious barriers which seemed to exist between all of us, in spite of our interest in one another's concerns.

By Monday, it became clear to me that I must talk to someone. The most level-headed person I knew was my Uncle Hugh. Unfortunately, since he was the main person concerned, the situation was a bit delicate. More important, since I knew in advance that he would make light of the matter, this was really just a way of avoiding the issue. But I could not bring myself to take any more decisive action.

My opportunity came on Wednesday night. We had dined at home together, and spent the evening working. We finished what we were doing about eleven and sat talking, eating the sandwiches and drinking the whisky the butler had left on a tray in the library. Outside, it was wild with rain and a howling wind. In the library it was peaceful, the leather-bound books gave off their usual, peculiar musty odour, and ordinary political strife itself seemed a world away—let alone violent death.

I became aware that I had not answered my uncle's last remark and looked up. He was smiling at me faintly. "You've something on your mind, Christy."

It seemed as good a time as any. "Yes," I said. "I have—though I know you'll laugh. It's these things that have happened to you lately. Did you ever think—what if they aren't purely accidental?"

My uncle looked at me as if I had suddenly begun to speak in an unknown tongue. "You're serious, Chris?"

"Yes."

"A blowout, a strong reaction to digestive pills or to the accident— my dear Christy!"

"Yes. I know. But supposing—just for the sake of argument—that they had been—arranged?"

"You are asking me seriously to assume that someone is trying either to injure me or even to murder me? It's not like you to be so melodramatic, Chris. You've always been level-headed. Now if it were Daphne——"

"I know. But even so—do you know of anyone who would dislike you enough to want to injure you—or even to murder you?"

My uncle made an impatient sound. "Any man who's made a lot of money and been in politics is bound to make enemies. Do I know anyone who hates me enough to take steps—to injure or to kill me—no, I don't. The idea's preposterous, Chris. This is England—not Corsica."

I did not answer at once. Finally, I said, "I know. But the war's not been over so long that people trained to violence or used to violence have forgotten all about it."

"It's a more violent world than it was twenty years ago. Perhaps England's more violent than it was even ten years ago. I'll grant you that. But even so, we don't go in for assassinating our business or political rivals here."

"Not ordinarily."

My uncle gave me a shrewd glance. I could not tell what he was thinking. "What is it, Chris? What are you trying to say?"

"No more than I've said. Except—you never have been ordinary. Some people think this Freemen of Britain isn't ordinary either."

Nothing changed in my uncle's face. "What do they think it is?"

"They're not sure."

"But they're sure it's not something ordinary?"

"Let's say they have never known you to be associated with anything ordinary."

The clock boomed out midnight. The fire was dying down, and it was chilly in the library. My uncle said, "You hear things here and there, is that it? How much of it could you trace back to your cousin Giles?"

"I don't know," I said. "I saw Giles last week. He said something very indirectly—but nothing directly."

"He follows my movements with great care," said my uncle. He did not seem perturbed by this thought. Nor did his next remark cause him any worry. The fact it expressed had been familiar to all of us for too long. "You would have thought his extraordinary dislike for me would persuade him to find other objects of interest."

For once, I spoke without thinking. "He's so much like you."

"Like me?" My uncle was amused and his surprise was genuine. "Christy, you need a vacation. I cannot remember more than one or two subjects—unimportant ones, at that—upon which your cousin and I have ever agreed."

So we left it. I had spoken unguardedly, but I meant what I said. My uncle was not an intellectual; Giles was. My uncle was almost a dandy in his dress; Giles did not own one really good suit. My uncle had been in the War Ministry and had refused a seat in the Conservative Cabinet; Giles was a violent, Left-wing Socialist. But they both loved power. This passion which they shared of course drove them apart rather than together.

My talk with my uncle therefore accomplished nothing. I did not convince him that he might be in danger, and I gained no reassurance myself. I did not look forward to the party at Feathers with any pleasure.

The week-end started off inauspiciously. First, Charles telephoned from Paris to say that he had become tied up in something rather important and didn't think he could get to Feathers before Sunday morning. I then had to wait for some things to be delivered from the shops, and they were late. I drove down to Feathers to find that my aunt had once more tried to issue a few orders to my uncle's housekeeper, Mrs. Rapp, who was consequently in a very bad temper. By the time I had calmed her, dealt with various domestic matters, and eaten a hasty lunch, I took an extremely gloomy view of the coming party.

But by the early afternoon, things brightened. Mrs. Rapp recovered her normally even temper and the weather, which had been chilly and rainy, improved steadily. I went for a walk before tea and looked at the greenhouse, the gardens, and the tennis courts.

As I walked there by myself, recollections of my childhood came back to me vividly. Looking back, things seemed to have been very simple and pleasant, at least compared with the way they were now. I could remember a picnic one summer—I must have been about twelve. Charles was sixteen and had his first girlfriend. We were all teasing him about her. He was being very aloof and superior, but his eyes were shining with excitement. Timmy was playing some absurd game with Giles, and I remembered how gentle Giles had been with his younger brother. (Timmy had been killed in France in 1940.) It was all a long time ago.

My nostalgia was interrupted by the arrival of Daphne and Robert for tea. But I was left in rather a good mood, and the strain of the last few weeks seemed to have lifted somewhat. Anne came in just as we were finishing tea, and we were still talking children and the virtues of various schools when the others—Uncle Hugh, Uncle William and Aunt Mildred, Andrew, and Tay—arrived at about six. We all had drinks before going off to dress, and the general mood was easy and gay.

Because of this evidence of good humour, the evening went off well. Dinner was very good, and we spent the evening listening to the wireless, gossiping, and playing bridge. By midnight, when I went to bed, I was almost reconciled to spending three nights under the same roof with my Aunt Mildred.

Technically, as my uncle's hostess, I felt responsible for the guests in his home. However, as they were all relatives—except Tay, and he almost counted as one since he required no more attention than they did—I felt they could amuse themselves during the day. So I slept late and had breakfast in bed. When I came downstairs about 10.30, Aunt Mildred had gone into the village, Daphne, Anne, Bob, and Andrew had gone off to play golf. Tay was out for a walk. Uncle William had disappeared somewhere and Uncle Hugh was working in the library. After a few minutes with Mrs. Rapp, I went to see if my uncle needed me for anything.

I rapped on the library door and went in. Uncle Hugh was talking on the telephone. He sounded curt, and he had an odd look on his face. As I entered, he was saying, "No. I've got it. I'll see to it immediately. Don't worry." He hung up, and then, seeing me, spoke to me in his normal voice. "Good morning, Christy. Everything all right?"

"Yes," I said. "I came to see if you needed me for anything."

"No—there's no work for you. But there is one thing. I've got a young man coming. He'll be here by lunch-time and he'll probably stay over till Monday. Tell Mrs. Rapp, will you?"

I was somewhat surprised that my uncle had invited a stranger to what was essentially a family party. But I supposed it must be for some important reason. I said I would arrange things. "What's his name, by the way?"

"Donald Gresham."

I happened to be crossing the front hall when Donald Gresham arrived, so I introduced myself. He was a young man—about thirty—and he spoke with a slight North-country accent. I guessed him to be the product of some local grammar school, and to be working in an office or a bank. He was rather ordinary looking. But he had a very attractive voice, and his eyes were the dark, passionate eyes of the fanatic. Though I guessed, both from his clothes and from his manner, that he was not used to luxury, he did not seem especially self-conscious at being at Feathers, and he was very polite.

I took him along to say hello to my uncle before showing him to his room. My uncle said he would look after his guest, and I went out. I did not see either of them for the rest of the morning.

When I went into the library, where we generally had drinks just before lunch, I found everyone there but my uncle and Mr. Gresham. Aunt Mildred asked where my uncle had gone—she thought he had been working in the library.

"He was. But he's invited a man for the rest of the week-end. Donald Gresham. I imagine Uncle Hugh's showing him round now."

"Invited a man here for the rest of the week-end? Really, Christy, you might have told us."

"I didn't know till I came down this morning. Anyway what's it matter?"

"On a family occasion——" began my Uncle William.

"Do you know who he is, Chris?"

"No I've never heard of him. Do any of you know him?"

No one did. But I was aware of some tension in the room that had not been there before. If no one had met Mr. Gresham, someone— or several people there—suspected something about him. I looked around at the faces so familiar to me. They told me nothing.

Uncle Hugh and his guest came in shortly, and after general introductions, we all went in to lunch. The conversation went along smoothly, but the ease of the night before had gone. I was sure that everyone was thinking about Donald Gresham: what was he doing at Feathers and what was his connection with Uncle Hugh? Everyone was polite, but the unspoken questions seemed to hover in the air.

Nor was curiosity the only thing in the atmosphere. There was something else. I recognized it easily: hostility. It seemed to me so palpable that I almost felt I could touch it. I often sensed the unspoken hostility when the members of my family were together. I had become used to it. But there was something new to-day. It could be because it was directed towards the unfamiliar Mr. Gresham. But that was not all. There was another element. Someone was under pressure who normally contributed little to the family *malaise*. Robert? Daphne? Anne? As I looked at them now, I had the feeling that they all looked different somehow—more troubled or more intense than usual.

The butler, Sanderson, was passing the sweet. I helped myself and when I again looked at the faces of my cousins, they seemed as normal as ever. Uncle Hugh had told some story, and they were all laughing. I felt very much relieved. My over-active imagination had evidently produced something that was not there. Uncle Hugh told another story, I joined in the general laughter, and lunch ended a good deal better than it had begun.

In retrospect, I remember little of that afternoon. It rained off and on, and most of us stayed in the house. Uncle Hugh and his guest spent their time in the library. Tay read a book, and Andrew went for a walk. In spite of my efforts, my Aunt Mildred ran me down and insisted on talking to me. After a good deal of fruitless speculation about Mr. Gresham—in which I declined to join—she asked me in a solemn voice whether I knew that Giles had been seen in the neighbourhood lately. I have often wondered why some branch of Intelligence did not recruit my aunt. She would have been a very efficient spy. I hesitated, not wishing to discuss Giles with her, and finally said I had heard something about it.

"Then you know he's keeping a woman down here?"

"He's not keeping a woman," I said. "She's a painter. She has a cottage in Redcot. I suppose he comes down to see her."

"It's a disgrace," said my aunt.

"For Giles to have a girlfriend?"

"Don't be absurd, Christy. You know what I mean."

"No," I said. "I don't. Giles is of age, and at liberty to do as he pleases. It's none of our business."

"Giles is a member of this family. Of course it's our business. But for him to deliberately insult us by keeping a woman in our own village——"

"You don't know that he's keeping her," I said, wearily. "I've told you it's her cottage. And Redcot's not our village. Now you really must excuse me. I've rather a lot of things to do."

I managed a period of comparative peace until tea-time. But I had not heard the last about my cousin Giles. After tea, my Uncle William approached me solemnly and said he wanted a word with me about a private matter. There was no escape, so we went into the small sitting-room on the ground floor and I asked what it was about.

"It's about Giles."

"Oh, *no*," I said, before I could stop myself.

My uncle looked at me coldly. "I'm aware that you have already had a conversation with your aunt about him, Christy. She felt that you were very evasive with her and that you knew more than you were saying. After all, you do see more of Giles than the rest of us do."

"I see very little of him. And I know nothing more than I've said. I only heard some gossip—that he had a girlfriend and that she lived at Redcot."

"Giles is living with her. I've made some inquiries."

"You can't trust village gossip. In any case, what does it matter?"

My uncle said, "I don't think you have any sense of family responsibility at all, Christy. What Giles does reflects on all of us. But you never think of things like that. I dislike to bring up what must be a painful subject, my dear, but your own behaviour is a case in point. When you made that very unwise marriage, you consulted no one. That Fane boy—everyone knew how wild he was. And there were stories——"

I got up and walked out. I nearly knocked down Tay in the passage. He took me by the arm and led me into the light. "You look ghastly, Christy. What's the matter?"

"Nothing."

"You need a drink. Come along and get one."

We found whisky in the dining-room and sat down. "I gather you don't want to talk," said Tay.

"No."

He smiled. "Well, remember one thing. There's only thirty-six hours to go."

I looked at him with relief. "That's the first cheerful thought I've heard all day."

At dinner, my Uncle Hugh was at his best. His best was extremely good. The tension in the room—our individual, private tensions and the general strain between individuals—was feverishly high. But Uncle Hugh either did not notice the general *malaise* that prevailed at the beginning of dinner, or else chose to ignore it. He was a charming and entertaining host, and he carried us all with him. I remember reading about charisma when I was studying political science at Cambridge. I have never seen a better illustration of it than my Uncle Hugh that night.

The next morning, I was awakened by Charles. His news was so shocking that I did not even ask him how or when he had arrived at Feathers. For he came to tell me that Uncle Hugh had died during the night.

IV

I came down to the library about half an hour after Charles had awakened me. Most of the others were already there, or came in soon after. They looked subdued and depressed. Donald Gresham sat apart from the others. He looked as if he had slept very little, and his eyes glittered with something that looked like hatred as he watched the others in the room.

When Charles came in, everyone turned to him with relief—and expectation. He had been with the doctor, and we assumed he would tell us the cause of Uncle Hugh's death. We had a general impression that it was heart failure; though when my aunt said this to me in the semi-audible voice she considered suitable for such an occasion, I remembered that the doctor had told me only a few weeks earlier that my uncle's heart was entirely sound. I remembered how often doctors were wrong. But I was conscious of a nagging uneasiness, and I as well as the others hoped that Charles would say the few words necessary to dispel any doubt.

But Charles didn't. To all questions, he replied evasively that the doctor was still in Uncle Hugh's bedroom, and that he had sent for another doctor to get a second opinion concerning the probable cause of death. I glanced at Gresham. His eyes had not lost their feverish glow, and he stared at Charles with avidity.

My Uncle William was displeased, and said so. He resented the fact that Charles had taken charge. My uncle suggested that as head of the family, he himself ought to have been consulted. He added that he had always thought Harmer, the local doctor, a fool, and that the doctor's present behaviour was a case in point. "It ought to be simple to diagnose heart failure. There's nothing difficult about that. And as a matter of fact, anyone knowing Hugh would have expected it. He never accepted the fact that he was getting on. Not that sixty is old— but it's old enough for a man to start taking care of himself."

That Uncle William was delighted to have outlived his successful younger brother, thereby surpassing him in longevity if in nothing else, was evident. But Charles did not reply, and an uneasy silence again settled upon the room. I was conscious of grief, and even more conscious of surprise and emptiness. I had never thought of Uncle Hugh as dying like an ordinary man. I had not been passionately fond of him. But I had always liked him, he had been good to me, and he had been one of the pillars on which my life had always rested. I felt very much alone.

From time to time, someone made a remark in a low voice. But conversation never became general. We waited for what seemed a long time, while the tension imperceptibly increased. Finally, Dr. Harmer came into the room. To everyone's surprise, the other doctor he had chosen to consult was Dr. Adams, the local coroner. I glanced at Charles, and he nodded very slightly.

Adams was a man used to taking charge. He did now. He said the usual conventional words of sympathy, and then added, "I've something rather awkward to tell you all. Dr. Harmer called me because he wasn't satisfied concerning the cause of Sir Hugh's death. The symptoms didn't suggest heart failure to him. They don't to me, either. In fact, without a very thorough examination, I'm afraid it will be impossible to determine the exact cause of death. From a superficial examination, there doesn't seem to be any reason why Sir Hugh *should* have died."

We all stared at him, trying to understand what his words meant. Aunt Mildred said, "I don't see—what *could* he have died of?"

"There are various possibilities. As I've said, we'll have to make a more thorough examination."

Tay said, in his precise voice, "You mean you want to do a complete autopsy?"

"Yes."

"But that's absurd!" Uncle William had again become the family patriarch. "I shan't permit anything like that. If you can't discover what my brother died of, we'll find a doctor who can."

It was then that Donald Gresham cut in, and his voice was high and excited. "*You* won't permit an autopsy! I'd like to see you prevent it. *We'll* see there's an autopsy! Of course Sir Hugh didn't die of heart failure. He was murdered—and by one of you. And you won't get away with it—not if I have to choke his murderer with my bare hands!"

Everyone stared at Gresham as if he had gone mad, and Dr. Harmer said, coldly, "Who is this young man?"

I said, "An acquaintance of my uncle's, Mr. Donald Gresham. He's been staying with us since yesterday."

Gresham turned to Dr. Adams. "I'm not surprised you can't find out how he died. But I'll bet you he was poisoned—and by one of them. And they're not going to get away with it. If you won't look into the matter properly, I'll take it up with the police."

By this time, everyone had begun to talk at once. Adams cut through the general clamour. "I am the coroner," he said, "so technically I'm in charge here. Can you tell me on what evidence you're basing those statements?"

"I knew Sir Hugh. He wasn't ill—he could have lived for years. His London doctor had just told him so. I tell you he was murdered by one of these people. Sir Hugh was very rich, and none of his relatives had any money of their own at all. The amount of money they'll cut up among them now he's dead—well, it's worth murdering for, if you're inclined that way—or if you need the money."

Uncle William, Andrew, and Robert started for him at the same time. Dr. Harmer stepped in front of Gresham and waved them back. "You'll gain nothing by that. Perhaps you'd like to amplify that statement, Gresham—always remembering that there are witnesses and that what you are saying may be slander."

Gresham said, "Yes, I'll amplify it. I'm a member of the Freemen of Britain. Sir Hugh was very active in it, though he hadn't let it be publicly known. But he had decided to support us openly—almost immediately. He was going to give a large donation to the organization. I came down here to talk about it. Sir Hugh didn't tell anyone why I was here or who I was. But anyone could have listened at the library door. We weren't talking in whispers. Perhaps some of them knew his plans anyway—or guessed. Any one of them might have gone to any lengths to stop his association with the Freemen, and to stop him giving us any money. You can try threatening me, but it won't work. I'll demand a police investigation of Sir Hugh's death—and with my organization behind me, I'll get it."

There was a heavy, bitter silence. Adams broke it. "I need hardly say that I do not take this young man's extravagant statements seriously. But it is true that there are certain things about Sir Hugh's death which are—difficult to understand. In order to stop this kind of slanderous gossip, I would suggest that I communicate with the Chief Constable. Naturally, I can't speak for him. But I think that, in view of Sir Hugh's position, the Chief Constable will probably put the matter into the hands of Scotland Yard immediately. I have no doubt that a proper investigation will soon dispose of the problem—and of this young man's remarks."

My Uncle William considered this a monstrous suggestion. "I cannot understand what prompted you to make it, Dr. Adams. We shall certainly not do anything of the sort. We'll call in my brother's regular physician, and he will undoubtedly be able to settle the matter in short order."

Charles looked at my uncle, and at Gresham, and then briefly at everyone else. "I'm afraid that won't do," he said, quietly. "These two doctors are not satisfied about my father's death. Mr. Gresham has made some challenging statements. No one here has anything to hide.

I believe we must accept Dr. Adams' offer to get in touch with the Chief Constable. Like him, I believe that Scotland Yard will be called in, and that they will be able to clear up the matter very quickly." He turned to Gresham. "I shall expect you to withdraw your remarks—if they turn out to be unjustified—after the facts are known; and I warn you that you'll be in serious trouble if you make any unsubstantiated statements in the future."

My Uncle William started to object. But Charles' air of authority was so genuine that no one, not even Gresham, challenged it. Adams went to telephone the Chief Constable and to arrange for immediate (local) police guards to be placed both inside and outside the house. The rest of us dispersed slowly, in unhappy silence.

I went to the kitchen to try to make some domestic arrangements with Mrs. Rapp. She was evidently very much upset, and had been crying. We spoke together for a few minutes, but she had made very sensible plans about meals and there was little to discuss. As I came out of the kitchen, I met Charles and we strolled out into the garden together.

I remembered Paul saying to me, the night we had met Giles, "Your cousin Charles always seems to be playing a part." I wondered what part he was playing now. I could get no clue to what he was thinking from his face. But I was sure that he had not accepted Dr. Adams' offer with such alacrity just to silence Gresham's hysterical outburst. I said, "Charles, you know more than you said in the library. Why weren't they satisfied with Uncle Hugh's death? Did they think he had been murdered?"

Charles glanced at me. "The idea doesn't seem to shock you as much as it did everyone else. It's a point I've meant to take up with you. But you're quite right. I do know more than I said in the library, though perhaps it was unwise of the doctors to tell me. You see, Christy, they think my father died some time after two o'clock—say about two-thirty or so. He seems to have got out of bed for some reason—probably he went into the bathroom—and then to have collapsed on the floor and died. But there are no symptoms of heart failure and none of a stroke—no head injuries—nothing of any kind. So, quite correctly, Harmer thought it warranted looking into. He thought perhaps he'd overlooked something. But Adams found the same thing—or rather, found nothing. I think they'd have felt an investigation was needed, even if Gresham had said nothing at all."

"But you can't die from no cause. And as for Gresham's idea of poison, surely they could have scotched that right off? There's no poison that can kill without a trace."

"No," said Charles. "But there are poisons you'd need an autopsy to discover."

"Do you mean you think he was poisoned?"

"I honestly have no theories. But, as you say, you can't die of no cause. Scotland Yard has excellent pathologists. We'd better reserve judgment until we hear from them—assuming, as I do, that the Yard is called in. I now come to the other point I've wanted to take up with you. I've been talking to Raikes. He says he doesn't think that motorcar crash was an accident. He thinks the tyre had been tampered with, and he told me how he thought it had been done. He also said he talked to you about it. He very tactfully said he didn't know what you had made of it. But he thinks it could have been an attempt at murder."

"Raikes' professional pride was hurt because he had a blowout," I said. "He thinks it in some way reflects on him."

"I agree that's very likely," said Charles. "Still, did it occur to you to mention the matter to someone?"

"Yes. It did. I told Uncle Hugh. He said, 'My dear Christy, it's not like you to be melodramatic.'"

"Naturally," said Charles. "He would. You didn't think of telling anyone else?"

"I thought of it. The trouble was I couldn't decide whom to tell. You see, the car was all right on Saturday and it didn't go out of the garage on Sunday. All of you—and Tay—were at the house on Sunday. Anyone could have walked out of the house and into the garage—and back again—without causing comment or even being noticed. Whom would you suggest I should have consulted?"

"Yes. I see it was a problem. Did you really think any one of us capable of murdering my father?"

"Any one of you," I said, "or none."

"And that pleasant but not really necessary telephone call to Paris last Sunday? Was that in any way connected with worry about my father?"

I had no wish to go into the matter of Uncle Hugh's digestive upset and my near-panic on hearing of it. "No," I said.

"I agree that it was delayed reaction," said Charles. "If it was because you were worried, you should have called some days earlier unless—did anything else happen, Chris? Was anything else bothering you?"

"No," I said again.

Charles did not look entirely convinced. But he dropped the matter. "Do you think my father was murdered, Chris?"

I did not reply immediately. "*Do* you?" he repeated.

"I think it very likely. Do you?"

"I also think it very likely. And the burst tyre—do you think that was an unsuccessful attempt at murder?"

"I don't know," I said. The conversation was making me acutely uneasy. "And even if it was, there's little anyone can do about that now."

"You mean it's too late for the police to find any evidence? You'd be surprised. They'll go over that episode and everything connected with it with a fine-tooth comb. One thing though: you'll be less of a suspect than the rest of us. It's hardly likely you'd have damaged the tyre if you were going to be in the car. Have you any nomination for First Murderer, Chris?"

The question came out abruptly. "Not offhand," I said.

"And motives?"

"Gresham gave you a good motive this morning: money."

"Did anyone need money that badly?"

"I don't know."

"Besides," said Charles, "you're forgetting one thing. We've assumed that my father's left us each something. But no one really knows, and we shan't know until the will's read. Would anyone—of us—be desperate enough to murder on an assumption?"

"If he needed money badly enough—and were unbalanced."

"Yes," said Charles. "Christy, what about this Freemen of Britain? Do you know how deep my father was into it?"

"No. I tried to talk to him about it a few days ago, but he wouldn't."

"How did *you* learn about it?"

"Oh, rumours were getting around. I put a few things together. It all added up. He didn't deny it when I suggested it and I'm sure he would have if he'd had no connection at all with them. How did *you* hear of it?"

He could easily have said he had heard from Gresham that morning for the first time. He didn't. He said, "Rumours cross the Channel, too. I'd heard quite a bit—enough to convince me he was in very deep, or would be soon."

"Is that why you came back last night instead of this morning, as you'd planned?"

"How did you know I came back last night?"

"You woke me before nine. I don't know a plane that gets you to London early enough in the morning for you to get to Feathers before nine."

"You're quite right. I finished earlier than I expected, so I came back last night—got here just before midnight. I didn't want to wake anybody, but when I went up to my room, I saw a light under my father's door. So I went in."

"To wish him a happy birthday or to talk to him about the Freemen?"

"Both. He didn't talk much about the Freemen, but I certainly got the idea he was going to back them very heavily, and that he'd been working with them closely already."

"What did you tell him?"

"Contrary to what Giles would expect, I tried to dissuade him. He said we'd talk of it again. But I had the idea he'd made up his mind."

"Then Gresham was probably telling the truth this morning about what Uncle Hugh planned to do?"

"I think so."

"Would anyone murder him because of that?"

Charles' eyes met mine. They were entirely without expression. "Well, it's either that or money, isn't it? I can't think of another reason."

V

Dr. Adams had acted very quickly. So did the Chief Constable. As Dr. Adams had expected, Scotland Yard was called in almost immediately. By six o'clock that same evening, the pathologists had determined the cause of Uncle Hugh's death, and the Scotland Yard Inspector, a man named Burgess, was talking to all of us in the library.

The atmosphere in the room was tight and strained. Daphne sat with her hand in Robert's, and Anne and Andrew, together on the sofa, occasionally murmured something to one another in low voices. Tay sat alone and seemed as withdrawn as he had been all during the week-end. Uncle William looked shattered, and I realized that in spite of his remarks in the morning, he had been profoundly unsettled by his brother's death. Like all of us, after all, he had been propped up by Uncle Hugh all his life. Donald Gresham sat aloof and withdrawn. No one spoke to him. And Charles lounged near the fire, his hands in his pockets, looking like a Hollywood conception of a young English diplomat. That, I gathered, was his present role. But in spite of his almost consciously graceful pose, his eyes were alert and watchful.

Burgess was a quiet, pleasant-spoken man about forty-five, obviously well educated and entirely at ease in his surroundings. He had clearly been picked with some care for this job. He began by expressing formal regrets to the family for Uncle Hugh's death, and was then introduced to all of us by Dr. Adams. Then Burgess took over again.

"I'm very much afraid that I have to tell you Sir Hugh did not die a natural death. I find it impossible, for various reasons, to avoid the conclusion that he was wilfully murdered."

There were one or two exclamations, but Burgess' authority held the room quiet as he went on. "It will therefore be necessary for me to conduct a regular police inquiry into his death. I am certain that all of you will be co-operative. My men will try to be as unobtrusive as possible—and I shall try to be as quick as possible."

There was another pause, broken by Andrew. "Do you think we could be told how he was killed?" he asked.

"Yes," said Burgess. "He was killed because he was given a new drug which lowers the blood-pressure very markedly. They discovered Sir Hugh had been given it when they did a gastric analysis. The drug was probably in tablet form—it dissolves very easily. It was, I believe, put in the water carafe that stood on his bedside table. He got out of bed, probably to go into the bathroom, and there was just not enough blood reaching the head to enable him to go on functioning. He fell into a faint and never recovered consciousness."

The cold matter-of-factness stunned all of us. Andrew said, "You're sure?"

"Quite sure."

"And the drug—the name of it, I mean?"

"It's a relatively new one—used in treating hypertension. It's called hexamethonium bromide. It's not too easy to come by."

There was an appalled silence. Then Andrew said, in a slightly unsteady voice: "It's odd that it should be just that drug. You see, we all—know about it. We were talking about it at a family dinner some months ago. Our own London doctor—his name's Barker—was there. He was one of the pioneers in its use, and he was telling us about it."

We sat like statues. Burgess said: "You all have the same doctor in London?"

"Yes."

"And that dinner-party was some months ago. How many months? Three? Six?"

Charles pulled a diary out of his pocket and flicked through it rapidly. He gave Burgess the date. It had been nearly five months ago.

"Have any of you been to see Dr. Barker at his office since then?"

Silence again. I said: "I had." And gradually, everyone else admitted that at some time or other during the past five months, he had been to the doctor's office in Harley Street. Gresham, of course, had not. He added that he had never heard of the drug, and I think most of us believed him. The possibility that any of the servants had had access to such an uncommon drug, or that having had access they would understand its characteristics, was limited. It was difficult to escape the conclusion that one of us in that room had murdered my uncle.

Burgess having, I imagine, learned more than he had expected, went on to his next point. Had any of us, he asked, been in Sir Hugh's room any time during the previous evening?

There were again uneasy glances and silence. Then my Aunt Mildred said brightly that she just remembered she had gone to talk to Sir Hugh before dinner. Burgess asked courteously whether her errand had had any particular purpose.

My aunt's reply, stripped of its verbiage, was that she had gone to see Sir Hugh about the inefficient way his household was run and in particular about the failure of the housekeeper, Mrs. Rapp, to model her behaviour on my aunt's wishes. Aunt Mildred indicated that though her niece, Mrs. Fane, was supposed to have some responsibility for the household, she appeared to meet this responsibility by allowing the servants—and particularly Mrs. Rapp—to do precisely as they pleased. Andrew gave me a rather wan and apologetic grin at this, and Charles winked in sympathy. But Burgess listened to my aunt impassively and asked how long she had been with Sir Hugh.

"But I didn't see him," said my aunt. "When I went in, he had already gone down to dinner."

What that meant—though I don't suppose Burgess realized it then—was that my aunt, finding my uncle away, had taken the opportunity to scrutinize those of his belongings and possessions which he had left lying around the room. It also meant, I guessed, that she had been seen by some maid going into the room. Otherwise, whatever her intentions had been, she would not have volunteered any information about her visit to Sir Hugh's room. These uncharitable reflections were the result of long knowledge of my aunt, and of her mixed feelings toward Uncle Hugh. I did not believe she had hated him enough to kill him; but if she had thought his death would benefit herself or her immediate family, I doubt whether she would have been troubled by many scruples.

"He went down fairly early," said Anne, "to have a drink. I was early, too, and I rapped on his door on my way. I wanted to ask him if he'd come to dinner later in the month—there were some people who'd particularly wanted to meet him. I stayed in his room talking for a few minutes, and then we went down to the library together."

Anne's self-possession seemed to suggest that any additional questions would be unnecessary. Burgess seemed to agree, for he turned to listen to my Uncle William. "I went upstairs with Hugh," said my uncle, "and I spent a few minutes with him in his room. We were talking about the business—just general things, you know. And as I came out," he added, with a triumphant look, "I met Mr. Tay. He was just going in."

"That's right," said Tay. "Like you, I wanted to discuss some points about the business. I didn't stay long, either—about fifteen minutes."

"Perhaps we could put this on some sort of a time basis. What time did you all go upstairs?"

After a general discussion, it was decided that it had been about 11.15. Anne here interjected that she had gone up a few minutes earlier. It was established that Tay had met Uncle William on the threshold of Uncle Hugh's room at about 11.30 and had himself left about 11.45.

"That's much better," said Burgess. "It's easier to work when one has some idea of the time involved. Now, did anyone else go into Sir Hugh's room?"

Charles and I spoke at once, and Charles deferred politely to me. "I went upstairs just after dinner—about 9.30. I wanted to make sure everything had been done by the maids for the night. I just opened the doors to all the rooms and gave a quick look. I didn't go in, though."

It is surprising how the fact of murder can make one's simplest and most natural activities sound sinister. It was as obvious to me as to everyone else that I could have put the tablets into the carafe at my leisure, on that entirely ordinary trip upstairs. I caught myself suppressing a desire to expand on what I had said, to explain that I did this customarily, though on Friday night, having been unusually tired, I had omitted it. But Burgess only took note of my statements as he had those of the others and waited for Charles.

But before Charles could speak, Andrew cut in ahead of him. I wondered if he had forgotten Charles' earlier attempt to intervene. "I went in to see him," said Andrew. "But I didn't see anyone else. It was quite late—a quarter to one, or just before."

Uncle Hugh had clearly spent a sociable night. Yet—had we not had the fact of murder to contend with—this was not so unusual. My uncle was known to work late or to read late, and he seldom went to sleep before two in the morning. Moreover, he was a difficult man to see alone, so that people with things on their minds might legitimately have cornered him in his bedroom late at night. It had frequently happened before. Burgess said, "And what did you go to see him about, sir?"

Andrew looked thoughtful. He was apparently debating with himself whether, as a matter of policy, he ought to follow Tay and his father in saying that he had gone to talk about the business. Then obviously coming to a different decision, he said, incisively, "I went to talk to him about the Freemen."

There were murmurs, and I saw Charles eyeing Andrew with mixed amusement and approval. Andrew certainly was a bit of a tough, I thought. He could easily have lied, since it was highly unlikely that anyone could have overheard his conversation with Uncle Hugh; and he had chosen instead to introduce the highly charged subject of the Freemen, about which everyone else except Gresham had been discreetly silent. Uncle Hugh, I thought with some amusement, would have behaved in exactly the same way.

"The organization the Freemen of Britain, sir?"

"Yes," said Andrew. "And I think you'd better hear the whole of it—rather than distorted part-versions. You see, my uncle had become very much interested in the Freemen—and you must have some idea what it's like. It's been called a Fascist organization, and I think that describes it well. He had decided to support it very strongly and openly—he'd been doing so privately for some time. I guessed he was planning to do something public and when he had Gresham here this week-end, I was sure. I thought the whole idea of the Freemen bad, and my uncle's association with it bad for himself, the family, and the business. I went in to tell him so."

I felt a relief at that blunt statement. It was better to have it out in the open. Charles had said two possible motives: money or the Freemen. Burgess now had both of them on a plate, and he could see what he could do with them. He said very politely to Andrew, "Thank you very much, sir. That's very helpful," and then turned to Charles. "Did you want to say something, Mr. Mason?"

"Yes," said Charles. "I got back late last night. I'd originally intended to come over from Paris on the early plane. But I finished earlier than I expected, and I don't like getting up early. So I caught a plane and got a car at the airfield to bring me down here. I arrived before midnight and came upstairs. I didn't want to bother anyone and I knew my room would be ready for me. But as I passed my father's door, I noticed light coming from under it and I knew he was still up. So I knocked and went in."

"I see, sir. You must have wanted to say hello and tell him you were here?"

"Partly that—and to wish him a happy birthday. But, like my cousin, I also wanted to talk to him about the Freemen."

Burgess seemed faintly surprised. "You'd heard about it in Paris?"

"In Paris, yes—and when I've been over here for a few days. I also thought it an unwise idea and an unwise association for him. To-day was his birthday, you know. We were going to have presents and speeches at lunch. My father rather liked occasions, and I thought it not unlikely he might pick the occasion of his birthday to make some kind of announcement of his plans. Once he'd done that, it was less likely he'd go back on it than if he'd never said anything to us at all. I wanted to talk it over with him first."

"And did you?"

"Yes. I put my point of view and he listened. But he wasn't convinced. I could see he wasn't going to be and I was tired anyway, so I didn't stay long. I don't suppose I was with him longer than fifteen minutes—twenty at the outside."

Well, I thought, he had certainly matched Andrew in bluntness. Burgess said to me, "Mrs. Fane, you worked closely with your uncle. Did you ever talk to him about the Freemen of Britain or did you know what he planned to do about it? Did you know anything about it at all?"

"I'd heard some rumours," I said, slowly. "I did speak to him about it once. That is, I spoke of his association with it. He didn't deny it, but he didn't seem to want to talk about it. I didn't know what his plans were, though."

If Burgess thought it unusual that though I worked so closely with my uncle in his political activities, I knew so little about such an important interest of his, he did not say so. "Did you also disapprove?" he asked.

"Yes."

"If he'd openly associated himself with the organization you would have stopped working for him?"

"Yes."

"Did you tell him so?"

"No. But I'm sure he would have expected it."

Tay appeared to be engrossed in his own thoughts. But he answered readily enough that he agreed with all of us. He had known that my uncle had had some connection with the Freemen, but had not been sure of its exact nature. My uncle had been evasive when the subject was mentioned. Like Charles, Tay considered the association unwise.

"And you, sir?" Burgess asked Uncle William.

Uncle William thought we were all making a great deal out of nothing. He'd heard Hugh's name associated with the Freemen, but he didn't really credit it. We had, after all, only Mr. Gresham's word for it that my uncle really contemplated anything so absurd as an open association with the organization, let alone giving it any substantial financial support. My uncle implied that he did not think much faith should be placed in Gresham's word. Hugh had a good deal of common sense when it came to the point, and he thought that all of us, including Tay, had got the entire matter out of proportion.

Burgess again nodded, and asked if anyone else had known about my uncle's activities with the Freemen. Anne and Daphne and my Aunt Mildred all appeared to have heard of it, but nothing more. The two girls did not seem to have been much interested; and as my aunt had got her information from her husband, it seemed unlikely that it was very accurate. Robert said that he had known of it, though he had not realized how far my uncle had planned to go. He added flatly that though it was none of his business, he thought it an outlandish idea. Burgess then asked if any of them had been in my uncle's room the previous evening or night, and all said no.

I was somewhat surprised that Donald Gresham had said nothing so far. But he did now, in a voice shaking with anger. "I don't know about the rest of them," he said. "Myself, I wouldn't trust a word they said. But she"—he pointed at Daphne—"she went in to see him. It was after midnight. I saw her."

Daphne turned white as chalk. She started to speak, couldn't, and burst into tears. Her mother and Robert both tried to quiet her, while we all tried to look as if nothing were happening. When she had managed to control herself a little, Burgess asked Gresham how he had happened to see Daphne—if he had.

"I didn't go right to bed," said Gresham. "I had some work to do. Just after midnight, I remembered I'd left something in the library and I went down to get it. When I came back up, I saw her slipping into Sir Hugh's room. I was a little worried about him anyway. I guessed they'd got word of what he planned to do and I knew what they'd think of it. They've just told you. And if you don't think any one of them is capable of murdering him, after what they've just said——"

"That is what I shall attempt to find out," said Burgess. "Suppose you just tell me what you did next."

"Well, I went back to my room and went on with what I was doing. Then I began to get a bit windy. As I've said, I knew this lot was capable of anything. So I went down the corridor to his room."

"What time was that?"

"Oh, it was well after one by this time. Say twenty to two. The light was still shining under the door. I stayed in the corner near the stairs for a while. I don't know how long—maybe fifteen or twenty minutes. Then the light went out, so he'd obviously gone to bed. I stayed a while longer, but nothing happened, so I went back and went to bed myself."

"That would have been after two o'clock."

"Yes. That's right. I looked at my watch when I got back to my room and it was about ten-past two."

"Of course, we've only your word for that," said Uncle William. "How can you prove you didn't go and poison him yourself?"

The incongruity between this suggestion and his continued insistence that his brother had died a natural death did not seem to strike my uncle. Donald Gresham looked genuinely surprised. "Why should I? I'd nothing to gain and everything to lose."

Uncle William persisted. "How do we know you're telling the truth? Maybe my brother had told you he'd decided against doing anything at all and was pulling out of the Freemen—and you killed him?"

Gresham looked at him with amazement. "You heard what everyone else said," he pointed out. "And I can prove what he himself said to the two top members of my organization. Besides, he'd hardly invite me to a week-end at his home just to tell me he was pulling out, would he?"

"Mr. Gresham," said Burgess, "when exactly did Sir Hugh invite you down for the week-end?"

"Late on Thursday," said Gresham, promptly.

"Had you expected such an invitation from him—or were you surprised?"

"Well," said Gresham, a bit dubiously, "I don't know quite how to answer that. I hadn't expected it, no. But I wasn't surprised especially."

"Let me put it another way, Mr. Gresham. Apparently Sir Hugh had been considering making a public announcement of his support for the Freemen for some time. It wasn't a new idea—and it was going to be an important step. Presumably timing was important. Yet he invited you down on fairly short notice. This would seem to suggest that he suddenly decided to put forward the date on which he would make the public announcement. I don't claim that's what happened, of course. He just could have decided that an opportune moment had come. But it's conceivable that something happened which made him act more quickly than he'd planned. Have you any idea what it might be?"

Gresham looked astonished, but very much interested. "I don't know of anything, no. But you're right—we did think it was rather sudden. Still, Sir Hugh always knew what he was doing, and we thought there wasn't any reason why he shouldn't make the announcement fairly soon."

Burgess turned to the rest of us. "Can you think of anything that might have caused Sir Hugh to act suddenly instead of taking his time as he'd planned?"

No one could. Burgess said to Gresham, "I suppose that if the announcement of Sir Hugh's connection with the Freemen had come as a disclosure by someone else rather than as an announcement made by himself, it would have been less valuable for the organization?"

"I suppose so," Gresham admitted. "But I don't think in the long run it would have made much difference."

"Perhaps not. But if I'm right—then if Sir Hugh feared someone else might get in first—that would have been a good reason for his haste?"

Gresham agreed that it might be so. Again, Burgess did not labour the point. He just asked Gresham whether my uncle had said precisely what he hoped to do for the organization financially.

Gresham was not sure. "He didn't name a figure. But he did say he thought we'd need about £250,000 to get on our feet properly."

It was a large sum by anyone's standards. We all looked shocked, and Gresham looked pleased at his results. But Burgess took it calmly, and asked Daphne if she would now tell him about her visit to Uncle Hugh's bedroom the night before.

Daphne, in a very quiet voice, said that she had gone to see her uncle on a private matter. It had, as she put it, "nothing to do with anything". That was all she would say, and no amount of coaxing— chiefly by Aunt Mildred, as Burgess accepted at least temporarily her mulish silence—could get anything else out of her.

Finally, my aunt gave it up. "I don't know why you have to persecute Daphne," she said, though she was the only person who had. "If she wanted to go and talk to her uncle, she had a perfect right to. It's far more reasonable than Charles suddenly rushing back from Paris at all hours of the night, and coming into his own father's house like a thief. And I'm surprised that no one's mentioned Giles. He's here in the neighbourhood frequently and he's probably here this week-end. If Charles could walk into the house unnoticed, so could Giles. And if anyone hated Hugh—which considering all Hugh had done for him is downright wicked—Giles did. And he's got an ungovernable temper—always did have, even as a child. If I were you, Inspector, I'd investigate his movements very carefully indeed."

It would have been difficult to surpass the sheer malice of that speech. Aunt Mildred's dislike for all of them—Hugh, Charles, and Giles alike—was so patent that it even shocked me, and I had been aware of it all my sentient life. I wondered drearily if all families in fact were that way with each other under the surface, and if we—and especially Aunt Mildred—simply let it come out on the surface more than most people did.

Burgess said, "Mr. Giles Randall, that would be? I wasn't aware he lived here."

It all came out then: Giles' political beliefs, his girlfriend in Redcot, his general tiresomeness. It all poured out, while everyone else seemed to withdraw into themselves, and I tried to hear as little of it as possible. But finally Aunt Mildred ran out of information and stopped; and Burgess said he would not interrupt our dinner, but would like to see each of us in turn in the small sitting-room (where it had been arranged for him to work) as soon as we had finished.

Luckily, we were relieved of Gresham's presence. Burgess did not have to be told how an uncomfortable atmosphere would be made very much worse if Gresham remained. Nor did Gresham show any desire to stay at Feathers. While we were at dinner, he gave Burgess a more detailed account of his afternoon with Uncle Hugh and of the early hours of Sunday morning. His luggage and his room were both searched with care by one of Burgess' men. Gresham was then allowed to go off to the village inn, and Burgess no doubt saw to it that an eye was kept on his activities.

Dinner was an uncomfortable meal. There was very little conversation and no one seemed to look at anyone else. By the time it was my turn to see Burgess, I was so glad to escape from my family's company that I almost didn't mind the coming interview.

Burgess' first questions had to do with my arrival at Feathers, with Friday night and Saturday morning, and with domestic arrangements. He then switched to the arrival of Donald Gresham. "Did it strike you as unusual that Sir Hugh should suddenly introduce a stranger into a family party without any explanation?"

"It did, rather."

"When the others found out about it, how did they react?"

I remembered the scene in the library and my uncomfortable awareness of hostility at lunch. "They seemed a bit surprised at having a stranger suddenly thrust upon them."

"Did anyone appear to know him?"

"No."

"But you guessed who Gresham was?"

"I guessed he was connected with the Freemen, of course. It seemed the only logical explanation."

"Judging from what was said, the others must have guessed, too. Did anything unusual happen at lunch—or at dinner?"

"No. Gresham was very quiet and self-effacing. He didn't say much."

"Did your uncle seem in any way unusual? Depressed?"

"On the contrary. He was very cheerful, almost exhilarated. I'd seldom seen him in such a gay mood."

"You guessed he'd come to some decision about the Freemen?"

"I thought it might be that."

"He didn't strike you as a man contemplating suicide?"

"Not possibly."

"He doesn't sound the sort of man who would commit suicide under any circumstances."

"I don't think he was."

"All right," said Burgess. "Now tell me about money. I understand that the contents of your uncle's will aren't known to any of you?"

"That's right."

"And none of you had any capital of your own. You just had such money as Sir Hugh chose to give you?"

"That's true as regards Uncle Hugh's money. I mean, Robert Alison and Andrew's wife, Anne, have some capital of their own. And, of course, Uncle William has quite a bit of money."

"Which I understand he made through his brother's offices?"

"Yes."

"Though Mr. William Mason is, as you say, well-to-do, his wealth isn't in the same class with his brother's?"

I agreed.

Burgess then asked about my own financial arrangements with my uncle, and commented that they seemed very generous. "Was he as liberal with his own son or with your other cousins?"

"I honestly don't know. I couldn't even guess what he did about Andrew and Daphne. I don't see any reason why he should have been any less generous to Charles than he was to me."

"He was angry with him for going into the Foreign Office instead of into the business?"

"If he was, he never said so, and he never acted as if he were. I've always thought he approved. But it's only a guess."

"He liked the nephew who's in the business, Andrew?"

"I believe so."

"More than his own son?"

"I suppose Uncle William told you that. Well, I don't know, and what's more, Uncle William doesn't know either."

"He did suggest it," admitted Burgess, smiling slightly. "Well, let's complete the list. He liked Mrs. Alison? Her husband? Andrew's wife? Mr. Tay?"

"All of them," I said, briefly. "At least, so far as I could judge. He wasn't a man who went in for very intense personal relationships."

"But he must have felt intensely about your other cousin."

"Giles? I suppose it seems so—and yet, do you know, I don't think he did."

"He—Mr. Randall—wouldn't stand to profit by Sir Hugh's death?"

"You mean, would he be left any money? I should say the chances were against it. But it's not entirely impossible."

"Do you think your uncle might have left him some money hoping to wean him back to capitalist ways?"

We both laughed. "Giles was brought up in capitalist ways and look at him. Besides, if the possession of money alone makes capitalists, Giles would be one. He makes a great deal of it."

"Your aunt," observed Burgess, "seems to feel that your cousin's political differences with your uncle were a very serious matter indeed. Some of their differences, of course, were common knowledge."

It was a difficult remark to reply to. "It's true enough they saw things very differently. It's always difficult to say how deep these things go."

"Did your cousin Giles know about your uncle's association with the Freemen? As he was a journalist, I suppose he must have."

"He probably did," I said, cautiously. "Of course, he wouldn't be in sympathy with the aims of the Freemen."

Burgess smiled. "That's one way of putting it. They're rather a mixed crew, your cousins, aren't they? Mr. Andrew Mason, now—I gather he and your uncle's assistant, Mr. Tay, weren't very friendly? Some rivalry in the business?"

Either Burgess had done a good deal of research into family matters before coming down to Feathers or else these matters were more widely known than I had suspected—or else he had picked up an incredible amount in his short time in the house. He might, of course, have got much of it when seeing the servants, which he had done before starting on the family. I said briefly that he was correct.

"Was everyone aware of the situation between those two?"

"Everyone was aware there was a situation," I said. "No one knew exactly what it was or how things would turn out."

"It's odd none of you tried to mediate between the two."

"There are some things for which there aren't any solution," I said. "Both of them want to control the company. They aren't the type to work in harness with each other. It doesn't make any difference what anyone does. If one wins, the other loses. There isn't any room for compromise."

"There are situations like that," agreed Burgess. "Tell me, Mrs. Fane—had you ever, before your uncle's death, I mean—thought of violence in connection with your family?"

"Violence?" I repeated. "No. There was a certain amount of—well, as you've just said, the relations between Andrew and Tay weren't very good. And Giles and my uncle didn't get on. But they never saw each other, after all."

"Yet your uncle's chauffeur, Raikes, tells me that *he* suspected something odd. He wasn't satisfied with the explanation of that accident you three were in on the way to Birmingham a couple of weeks ago."

"No," I said, slowly, "I know he wasn't."

"He even made some investigations on his own—and told you about them, I understand. Didn't you take them seriously?"

I was reasonably sure that Raikes had not known about my uncle's indisposition in the Birmingham hotel, as he would have mentioned it to me. On the other hand, Dr. Barker did know, and was sure to mention it to the police. I could have told Burgess I had known nothing of this, but it might have sounded a bit thin. Besides, I remembered my conversation with Charles. He had quickly assumed that my apparently innocent telephone call to Paris the previous week-end had been in some way connected with my anxiety about his father. If he learned—as he probably would—of Uncle Hugh's illness in Birmingham, he would put the two things together without difficulty. Once he had, I rather thought he would tell Burgess, though I had no idea what his motive in doing so would be. I decided I had better tell the truth.

"I hadn't made up my mind," I said. "I listened to Raikes, of course. It was difficult to take seriously the idea that anyone was trying to harm Uncle Hugh. I think I worried for a day or two after I spoke to Raikes. But I was in bed, and not feeling very cheerful. After I'd been back to work for a few days, it all seemed a bit melodramatic—Raikes is a bit of a fusser, anyway—and I didn't consciously worry about it."

Burgess nodded. "Raikes told you his suspicions about the tyre pump having been used. I suppose he's neat enough so that we can at least say with certainty that someone moved the tyre pump—for whatever reason?"

"Oh, yes. He'd be right about that."

"Have you any idea why Raikes didn't proceed any further with his investigations?"

As I had already made the point to Charles, I could see no point in dodging it. "I don't know," I said. "But I can guess. You see, it would have been quite possible for anyone to use a skeleton key to get into the garage, or for a lot of people to use the key that hangs in the kitchen. But it happens that the Sunday night before the accident we had a family dinner. Everyone was there except Giles. And Tay came in later. I suppose Raikes thought the situation a little—delicate."

"Yes," said Burgess. "He might indeed. But you—you forgot about it or did nothing about it."

I hesitated. "I spoke to my uncle about it."

He pounced. "When? What did he say?"

"Wednesday night—last week. He said that I was being melodramatic and that it had been a simple accident."

"I dare say he would think just that. Perhaps you even knew he would say it when you spoke to him."

"I thought he might. He wasn't the sort to get alarmed. But maybe I hoped—it would put him on his guard."

"Then you *did* think there was danger? But why did it take you so long to make up your mind to say something?"

Again I hesitated. "Well, you see, I had more or less put Raikes' idea out of my mind. But it lingered a bit, in spite of myself. Then on Wednesday my uncle had a dinner-party and afterwards I saw him take a digestive pill. He told me he'd had a digestive upset in Birmingham and that the hotel doctor had been a bit puzzled by his symptoms. Our own doctor in London changed my uncle's pills after he returned to London."

I had kept my tone as carefully neutral as possible. Burgess was not deceived. "So you then decided that there might have in fact been two attempts made on your uncle's life. Is that it?"

"I wouldn't go as far as that. I was a bit worried, though—at least, concerned."

"But you did nothing?"

"Well," I said, "in an ordinary family like mine, one doesn't go round thinking of murder. I was a bit upset by Raikes' suggestion, but when I thought it over, it seemed far-fetched. When my uncle told me about his trouble in Birmingham, I again got alarmed, but I couldn't decide just what to do. And so—I suppose to reassure myself—I rang up all my relatives and talked to them."

Burgess appeared to understand without difficulty. "To convince yourself that they were entirely normal people and that your suspicions were ill-founded?"

"Yes."

"What excuse did you give them for ringing up—or do you do it normally anyway?"

"I said I'd called to confirm the final arrangements for this party."

"They all accepted this explanation?"

"All but Charles. That is, I didn't call my Aunt Mildred or my Uncle William. And Charles just said my calling was very thoughtful or something like that."

"But now he thinks it might have been prompted by something else?"

"Yes."

"He's very sharp, your cousin. What did he do in the war?"

"Intelligence," I said, briefly.

"On the Continent? Risky—cloak-and-dagger stuff?"

"More or less."

"Did you tell him about the digestive upset?"

"No."

"Why not?"

The continued questioning was beginning to be a strain. "I just didn't feel like it."

"Then why did you tell me? Because you thought I might learn it from Dr. Barker?"

"Yes."

"When you spoke to your uncle, you mentioned the digestive upset as well?"

"Yes. I asked what if both the episodes hadn't been accidental. But he brushed them both aside."

"You don't seem to have been very decisive about the matter, Mrs. Fane, if I may say so. Didn't you think of going to the police?"

It was a direct hit. I said nothing for a moment. Then I said that I had thought of it, but that I had hesitated to go to the police with nothing more than a few vague suspicions. I knew that it sounded weak. For Burgess knew and I knew that the police would have paid attention to anything involving a man like my uncle.

"Well, all right, Mrs. Fane, we have two possible attempts at murder. Let's look at the third. Saturday night. The rooms were made ready for the night while you were at dinner—this was the usual procedure?"

"Yes. When I went up on Saturday night at 9.30 or so, they had already been done."

"So I understand. Now, they tell me that each bedroom has a water carafe on the bedside table, that your uncle's was cut glass, with a stopper, and that the water is changed every night."

I was puzzled. "Yes. Is that important?"

"Yes," said Burgess. "Mrs. Fane, if we tested any carafe—say yours—for fingerprints yesterday, whose would you have expected to find on it?"

I considered. "My own, if I'd had any water. Anyone who'd come in to see me, if they'd had any water. And, of course, the maid's. Actually, they're supposed to dust the carafes every day and they usually do. But I suppose they might neglect it sometimes—which would mean fingerprints for a couple of days might conceivably be on it."

"The maid called Hawkins did the rooms last night. She was a bit rushed as there's been a lot of work and she was needed downstairs, so she hurried. She says she just took the tops off and filled the carafes— didn't stop to dust them. She's quite sure of it. But her fingerprints aren't on the stopper. So someone wiped it after she'd filled it. There is only one set of fingerprints on your uncle's carafe—his own. You can see what that means, I suppose?"

I could. It was not difficult.

"This third attempt," said Burgess. "At least, it could have been the third attempt. I'll have to learn what I can about the second from other people. But you can tell me a bit more about the first."

Burgess' idea of "a bit" proved to be intensive. We went over that dinner-party on Sunday night in exhaustive detail. I could remember most of what had happened; but it had all been very ordinary, and I could not see that it was much use to Burgess.

By the time we had finished with that episode, I was nearly dropping with fatigue. Burgess apologized for keeping me so long. "Only two small points, Mrs. Fane. First of all, most of the servants seemed most co-operative. But I had the distinct impression that one or two of them were holding something back. I can't quite put my finger on it and I've no idea what it might be. Do you think you might have a word with the housekeeper and suggest that—if she is holding anything back or knows anyone who is—she had better come and talk to me?"

"I'm sure they've all told you everything they can," I said, somewhat stiffly. "Mrs. Rapp is entirely reliable. I could hardly make a suggestion like that to her."

Burgess looked at me. He sighed. But he did not pursue the subject. Instead, he took from his pocket a small, amber cigarette-holder. "The maid found this in the corridor outside Sir Hugh's room early Sunday morning," he said. "She meant to give it to the housekeeper, but she put it in her pocket and forgot about it. When she learned Sir Hugh had been murdered, she thought it might be important and she gave it to me. Do you know whose it is?"

I examined the holder carefully. "I'm sorry," I said. "I'm afraid I don't."

I had not, however, told the truth. I knew quite well to whom it belonged. It belonged to my cousin Giles. He had been using it when I had last seen him.

VI

When I finally left Burgess, I felt at once over-stimulated and exhausted. It had been a long and wretched day. I didn't want to talk to anyone, so I went up to my room and went to bed. But I could not sleep, and finally I got up and took two sleeping-pills.

These put me into a very heavy sleep and I began to dream—vague and incoherent fragments of dreams that finally assumed a sequence. I was rushing, we were all rushing, and it appeared that we were afraid of missing our ship. We all made it, though: all of us at the house-party, and Giles, and Paul Meadows, and my old friend Lady Vicky and others I didn't know or couldn't remember. We all continued to run, this time round and round the deck. It seems to have been a race of some sort. Then we all had spears, we were carrying them in our right hands, grasped in the middle and pointing outwards. And then they were all chasing me, the spears outstretched, and finally they caught me and formed a circle of lethal points around me and I could not move. It was some sort of a trial. I don't remember exactly what I was accused of, but I knew I was innocent. I tried to say so, and opened my mouth to speak, but my voice was gone and I couldn't. I could see by their faces that they had found me guilty. I stood there helpless for a moment, and then broke through the circle and began to run.

I was on land now and running, with all of them in full pursuit. It had snowed heavily and was still snowing, and I floundered through the heavy, sticky snow. Then I was running up a kind of circular wooden staircase, with narrow, winding stairs. The snow was coming down thickly and the steps were slippery. I kept climbing up and up and the circle of stairs grew narrower and narrower, and suddenly I slipped and fell through the deep, thick, suffocating blankets of snow...

I gave a sudden, sharp jump in bed and woke. I was icy cold and shaking, and my forehead was wet. I woke with the mood of the nightmare still upon me, frightened and depressed. I looked at my watch—twenty minutes to six. The sleeping-pills had left me feeling heavy-headed, but I had no wish to go back to sleep. I put the bedside light on and tried to read. But I soon gave it up and just lay there quietly.

The day before had been so upset and confused that I had had little time to think about Uncle Hugh. I had the time now; and I thought with sadness of his unnecessarily early death. He was a man who had enjoyed life enormously. It was true, of course, that I had seen the best side of him. Those who had been the victims of his driving force or of his implacable egoism and self-confidence undoubtedly would feel differently about the matter.

I began to think of what my uncle's death would mean to me. In essence, it meant that I would have to reorganize my entire life—or rather, to organize it, since heretofore I had worked for him, lived in his house, and to a large extent regulated my life by his. At least, this had been the case for the past few years. Before that lay the war, now an almost forgotten interlude; and Cambridge and school and childhood. The future looked endless and without form. Yet somehow I had to find something to do with myself, some place to live, and something to look forward to. At six o'clock that morning, the difficulties seemed formidable. And when I thought of all that must come first—the investigation into Uncle Hugh's death, his funeral, the reading of his will, the arrangements about the town house and Feathers and the staff—my depression grew even more pronounced.

About eight, when the maid brought me my morning tea, I got out of bed, bathed, put on a dark costume and went downstairs. I was drinking coffee when Tay joined me at the breakfast table. He ate quickly and joined me when I left the dining-room to go into the library. No one else had come down yet.

I had known Tay nearly all my life. As far back as I can recall, he was always there, at Uncle Hugh's elbow. He was clever, self-effacing, reserved, and rather dry, with an enormous capacity for work and a shrewd business head. He had been Uncle Hugh's personal assistant for the best part of twenty years. So far as I could tell, it was a highly successful arrangement on both sides, though—since neither man was an emotional sort—I never thought it was a deep and devoted friendship. As I said to Anne, on one occasion when she invited me to lunch and tried to persuade me to talk about Tay and the business (Anne had asked whether I thought Tay really interested in what was best for the firm), "I'm certain he's interested in what's best for Tay. And what's best for the business *is* best for Tay."

My Uncle William and Aunt Mildred, of course, hated him. They were fanatically ambitious for their children and from the time Andrew had gone into the business they had expected him to take Tay's place with Uncle Hugh. My Uncle William was somewhat more realistic about the matter than my aunt. He knew how useful Tay was—and how firmly lodged in his place. So in the early days, my uncle satisfied himself with pinpricks and small jabs at Tay, but nothing more.

Then came the war. Andrew did very well, got a staff job, and finished with the rank of acting lieutenant-colonel. He returned to the business six years older, used to responsibility, and in no mood to resume his former junior role. Uncle Hugh, who was well aware of Andrew's ability, promoted him rapidly. But he did not make Andrew his personal assistant. Tay remained precisely where he was, aware of the situation and firmly entrenched. Andrew began to work quietly at dislodging him. And my Uncle Hugh watched it all, I presume; but he said nothing, and he did nothing.

Now there were in fact not one but two battles in progress or, more accurately, the struggle had two sides. Andrew wanted to supplant Tay as my uncle's personal assistant. But he wanted it chiefly because he felt it would put him in a good position to control the entire business after my uncle's death. And the crux of the situation was that no one had any idea—or so I believed—of how my uncle had left or divided the voting shares of the company. Once, when I was discussing it with Charles, I had said that Tay would be wise to try to manœuvre Andrew out of the business altogether, since if he did not, he was bound to lose. But Charles had disagreed.

"Because Andrew'll inherit some of the shares and Tay has very few?" he had asked. "Don't be too sure. My father can tie up control of that company any way he likes. It has nothing to do with the way he leaves his money. He might separate ownership from control completely. He could. Even supposing he divides his property among all of us, why do you assume we'd vote with Andrew rather than with Tay? Would you—if you came to the conclusion that Tay could run the business better than Andrew—and so make more profit for you?"

"I don't know. But with Uncle William and what Daphne will have and Andrew himself——"

"My father," Charles had said, "is incalculable. That is, in some ways. He's perfectly capable of encouraging a really vicious rivalry between the two of them—ostensibly on the theory that whoever wins out is better fit to run things. He's sixty—and it wouldn't surprise me to see him in active control still at eighty. I'm sorry for both of them. How lucky I was to select a career in the Foreign Office!"

I myself had always got along well with Tay. After I went to work for my uncle, I naturally saw him often. Occasionally we went out to dinner together, or to the theatre—Tay had never married. Tay's behaviour had always been very correct. He had not discussed the business with me and he had made no attempt to draw me into the struggle.

Naturally, the family did not believe this and saw what my aunt called "Tay's advances" to me as an attempt to enlist my support. They took various counter-measures. Anne invited me frequently to their country house. Daphne (whose mother was afraid I might be planning to marry Tay) was stimulated to try to introduce me to suitable husbands. (This campaign went on the rocks early because of our different interpretations of the word "suitable". Besides, the last thing I wanted was to marry again.)

None of this had escaped Tay. He had taken it all with equanimity. For all I know, he may even have enjoyed it. He had been somewhat quieter than usual this week-end and since my Uncle Hugh's death, his silence had become even more marked. Under present conditions, of course, he had a lot to think about.

We sat in the library not saying much for a few minutes. After a time, Tay asked me if I knew what arrangements were planned. "Burgess didn't give me any idea last night. Did he say anything to you?"

I shook my head. "I imagine we can have the funeral whenever we choose. Wednesday perhaps—and from here. But that's only a guess. It's really up to Charles to settle things, isn't it?"

"If he wishes to," said Tay, precisely.

"Well, if he doesn't, I presume he'll delegate someone else."

Tay agreed and seemed to lose interest. Abruptly, he changed the subject. "Christy, have you really no idea of the contents of your uncle's will?"

It was the first time he had ever discussed such a subject with me. Considering all the factors, I thought it a surprising question. "It would be much more logical for me to ask you that."

Tay smiled faintly. "I haven't. Ironic, isn't it?"

It was all of that. I said nothing, and Tay again changed the subject. "Christy—you're fond of Giles?"

"Fond of Giles? Why?"

"Let me put it another way. You'd protect him if you could?"

"Protect him against what?"

"Suspicion of murder."

"*Giles?*"

"Yes."

"I don't like conversational tennis," I said. "What are you trying to say?"

"That Giles was here in the house Saturday night. I heard him talking to your uncle. What's more, I heard him threaten to kill your uncle."

I did not bother to say that I didn't believe it. "Then why didn't you tell Burgess yesterday?"

"I was thinking whether I would or not. Let me put it to you, Christy. If Giles were known to have sneaked into the house last night, he'd be the most logical suspect—and not only because of his unconventional call. He's the one of you who's known to have hated your uncle. Motive and opportunity—the police would very quickly start searching for the means."

"Then why didn't you tell the police?"

"Several reasons. I'm very sorry your uncle's dead—on personal and other grounds. I haven't decided yet whether having his murderer caught and having a huge public trial and scandal would serve any purpose. It can't help your uncle any more, and I don't know that it can help anyone else. It certainly won't help the business."

"Then where does my protecting Giles come in?"

"I said I hadn't made up my mind. I was fond of your uncle and I don't like the idea of a murderer getting off scot-free. If I decide to tell the police, I shall explain the reason for my hesitation. I think they'll accept it."

"In short," I said, "if I do something for you, you'll decide not to tell the police you heard Giles on Saturday night."

"Exactly." He was as calm and as friendly as if we had been making plans to go to the theatre together. Yet the only correct name for what he was doing was blackmail.

"And that is?"

"That you vote your shares my way—instead of Andrew's." I stared at him. "But you don't know I have any shares!"

"No. But I'd guess you do. Your uncle liked you and he thought you had common sense. Anyway, it's a chance I'm willing to take. If he hasn't left you any voting shares, it's my loss."

"But—you've only my word I'll do it—if I do say yes. How d'you know I won't go back on it?"

"I don't know. But I don't think you would. As I've just said, it's my risk."

"Some people," I said, "would call this blackmail—a polite form of it, but blackmail just the same."

"And they'd be right," said Tay. "Do you imagine your uncle, in the course of making his fortune, hasn't done a good deal worse? Not to mention what he'd have been willing to do for the Freemen. Do you think Andrew would stick at something so small? Come, Christy— you're not naïve. You know all this as well as I do."

I did, of course. I felt heavy-headed and incapable of clear thinking. But I thought that at least I must see Giles before I refused Tay's offer. I said, "All right. I'll vote them your way," and left the library before he could say anything more.

Luckily, everyone seemed occupied with various concerns that morning. So about eleven o'clock I strolled unnoticed down to the greenhouse. There was a path near it which led down the hill, and one could find one's way over the fields to Redcot with a good chance of being unobserved. Once in Redcot, I found the cottage Bella had rented without much trouble.

Bella herself—there could be no mistaking her from the description Paul had given me—came to the door. She did not invite me in, but just stood there looking at me. "My name's Christina Fane," I said. "I've come to see my cousin Giles."

"He's not here."

"Then I'll wait. Perhaps I could wait inside."

She still stood in the doorway. "I don't know when he'll be here."

I said, impatiently, "Giles may be in trouble. I've come to see him about it. Now don't——" But at that moment, Giles himself came down the stairs and asked who was there, and Bella had no option but to say, "It's your cousin," and to let me in.

Giles was clearly surprised to see me. "And what brings you here?" he asked, after saying hello. His voice and his eyes were both wary.

"I want to talk to you—alone."

"You can speak freely in front of Bella. I don't have any secrets from her."

"Well, I do. I want to talk to you alone."

Giles stared at me a moment, and then asked Bella if she'd mind. She evidently did mind, but she went away and Giles and I were alone. He was wearing corduroy trousers and a pullover. He looked thinner than usual and rather pale—and more like Uncle Hugh than ever. I said, abruptly, "I came to ask you what you were doing in the house the night Uncle Hugh died."

His eyes met mine unblinkingly. "I don't know what you're talking about, Christy. I wasn't at Feathers. You're dreaming."

"The police have found your cigarette-holder," I said, bored. "It's only a matter of time before they find out whose it is. Furthermore, Tay happened to be in the corridor while you were shouting at Uncle Hugh—he heard you threaten to kill him. So you may as well give up that line."

Giles, not being a fool, did give it up. "You knew the cigarette-holder was mine and you didn't tell the police?"

"I haven't told them yet. I wanted to talk to you first. Tay hasn't told them for—well, for reasons of his own. Incidentally, from the unsurprised way you spoke of the police, it's apparent you know Uncle Hugh was murdered. *How* do you know?"

"Village gossip. I suppose it came through from the servants at Feathers. Anyway, it's an open secret around here."

It sounded reasonable enough. I said, "Is it also an open secret just how he was killed?"

"No," said Giles. "The stories seem a bit garbled. I gather, though, that he was poisoned."

"Do you know with what?"

"No. Do you?"

"Yes," I said. "But never mind that. Do you want to tell me what you were doing at Feathers on Saturday night?"

"I went to talk to our uncle. Why? You think I killed him, Chris?"

"I don't know. You could kill someone, I know that. And you hated Uncle Hugh enough for that. But whether you did or not—did you, Giles?"

"Hoping to surprise me into an admission? Naturally I'll say I didn't. I do say so. Do you believe me?"

I looked at his face. It told me nothing. "I thought if I saw you and talked to you," I said, slowly, "that I'd be able to come to some conclusion, one way or another. I can't. I just don't know." I paused. "What did you want to talk to him about? And why did you have to pick such an odd time?"

"I went to talk to him about his philosophy of life. I've been meaning to for some time. I was out for a walk and thought I'd stroll over."

"You can try telling that story to the police," I said, "and see how they like it."

"Are *you* going to tell the police?" I could not tell if his question was prompted by anxiety or by curiosity.

"I haven't decided."

"What I can't figure out," said my cousin, "is your motive in— shall we say, protecting me? And Tay's is entirely beyond me."

"You can work it out so that in some way it'll mean we're both exploiting the working class," I said. "On the surface, it looks an impossible connection. But I'm sure you'll find it."

He did not answer that. "I suppose things at Feathers are very lively—what with a murder, the civil war between Andrew and Tay, and Aunt Mildred's conversation. At least there isn't any political strife, is there? All good Tories together."

"Charles and I are not Tories. And even you can hardly believe I would discuss politics with Aunt Mildred."

Giles did not appear to have heard my answer. For he was smiling, a curious smile I had never seen before. It held an odd mixture of hate and triumph. He said, almost under his breath, something I could barely hear. It sounded like "or maybe not. You'd be surprised."

"What are you talking about?"

"Nothing. Of course, if you all get too bored with each other, you can always speculate on the contents of Uncle Hugh's will. I don't suppose you know what's in it yet, do you?"

"I don't. Do you feel he ought to have left you something?"

Giles looked angry. "Don't be an idiot, Chris. Of course he hasn't. It didn't even occur to me that anyone would think that."

"I wouldn't be too sure. Uncle Hugh had an odd sense of humour. And if he did—you'll refuse it with a fine burst of wrath, I hope. I'll be disappointed if you don't."

He did not answer. He came with me to the door, and I left him standing there, continuing to look like a much younger edition of the uncle he had hated and—as far as I could tell—would hate all his life.

The path over the hills to Feathers came into the village of Redcot not far from Bella's cottage. I had just turned into it from the road when I heard steps behind me and my name spoken aloud. I turned to find Bella. Though she had only walked the few yards from her cottage, she was breathing somewhat heavily and her face seemed very flushed. She said, "I'm sorry I was rude just now. You took me by surprise—I couldn't decide what I'd better do. But I want to talk to you."

"All right," I said. "What about?"

"About Giles, naturally. I listened to your conversation. I couldn't hear all of it, but I heard enough to know Giles may be in trouble and I'm worried about it."

"He very likely will be in trouble," I said. "But I don't see what there is to say about it."

"They *can't* suspect Giles of murdering his uncle."

"They seem able to suspect the rest of us. Why not Giles?"

"It's different for you."

"I don't see why."

"They'll handle you with kid gloves—you all being who you are. They'll be very careful with any evidence. But Giles—politically, he's outside the pale. All those people—the doctors, police, judges—they're worse than Conservatives, most of them—they're semi-Fascists. Giles wouldn't have a chance."

"You've been reading too many of Giles' articles," I said. "You mustn't believe everything he writes. I doubt if he does himself. Anyway, no one has to manufacture evidence that Giles was in the house Saturday night. He was."

She looked genuinely worried and though I didn't like her, I was almost sorry for her. It must have shown in my face, because she said, "I knew he'd been out that night. I didn't know he'd gone to Feathers. And he's been so odd ever since. I know he hated your uncle. He talks about him in jerky sentences, but he doesn't say much. He seems obsessed with him. I thought he'd be glad he was dead, but—I don't know. He seems more worried than anything else."

I couldn't think of anything suitable to say. "It's all a bit of a mess."

She stood there for another moment without speaking and then reverted to her earlier truculent tone. "Well, I just wanted to say—you can't lynch Giles. I'll see to that. He has powerful friends, too. Just remember that."

I checked my spontaneous response to that. The conversation seemed to have reached an impasse. Bella turned and went down the path and I continued on my way to Feathers.

When I came up the path near the greenhouse, I met Andrew. He asked where I'd been.

"For a walk. I got tired of Feathers."

"Have you been to see Giles?"

"No," I said.

"I don't believe you," said Andrew, flatly.

This rudeness was unlike him, and I looked at him carefully. He looked pale and drawn, and was obviously under great strain. One hand had a bit of sticking-plaster on it. I said, "What's wrong with your hand?"

"Cut it," said Andrew, briefly. "Don't bother to change the subject, Christy. I suppose it doesn't matter where you've been. But what I'm going to ask you now does. What were you talking about to Tay in the library this morning?"

"That also I believe is my business."

"You were making a deal with him—about the voting of control!"

"All this is a bit premature," I said. "How can I make a deal when I don't know I've inherited anything? How can anyone, for that matter?"

"You could make a provisional deal. You and Tay've been very thick anyway, for the last couple of years. My father warned me, but I never thought you'd favour a stranger over your family. However——"

I interrupted him. "I wish you'd stop jumping to conclusions. I have made no plans for anything so indefinite as the amount and kind of shares Uncle Hugh's likely to have left me. He's probably fixed up control of the company in his will anyway, and none of us will have much to say about it."

"I don't think so," said Andrew. "It's much more likely he wanted the struggle between us to go on. He'd think of it as a form of immortality. Well, he's dead now—and my sense of humour isn't his. But Chris—I don't think you're seeing this thing plainly."

He seemed much calmer now. I said, "What am I not seeing clearly?"

"The whole thing. If—as seems evident—Uncle Hugh was murdered, there was some good reason for it. And the person who had the good reason was the murderer."

"The person who had the best reason was the murderer," I corrected. "I suppose the police would think most of us had some kind of reason."

He said, impatiently, "Not strong enough to act upon. We were all his relations, after all. You need a strong motive to murder a member of your own family."

"And one not so strong if it's an outsider? I'm not so sure. You can hate the people you're closely allied to much more." I thought briefly of Simon. I wondered if one day I could have hated him. I had reason enough to, certainly. But one does not hate or love people for strictly rational reasons.

Andrew said, "I'm not sure people murder from hate. They murder for advantage. And the only person whose immediate advantage it was to have Uncle Hugh dead was—an outsider."

I said, "Tay? But why?"

"Well," said my cousin, "Tay's not young any more, and he's very, very ambitious. I ought to know—I've worked with him long enough. He wanted control and he wanted it now."

"But even if that's true," I objected, "how could he possibly be sure of getting control if Uncle Hugh died?"

"He couldn't be sure. But it was worth the gamble. I'm younger than he is. I can afford to wait. But he couldn't."

"All this is supposition," I said. "You could build up as strong a case against any of the rest of us." I thought fleetingly that you could build up an even stronger case against Giles.

"Part of it isn't supposition, though. Tay is certainly up to something. Look at what happened this morning."

"*What* happened this morning?"

"I forgot you weren't here. We were having coffee about eleven o'clock, when Daphne dropped her handbag. It opened and everything spilled out on to the floor. She rushed to pick it all up, but, of course, the rest of us did, too. She had a big packet of notes in her bag. Robert asked her where she'd got all that money and why she carried it around and she got upset and wouldn't answer. Then I looked at the notes. I recognized them right off. They were Uncle Hugh's—he'd drawn them at the business on Friday, just before we left. Everyone began to ask questions at once and Daphne got flustered. First she said Uncle Hugh had given them to her and then she said Tay had. Tay said he hadn't. Burgess tried to break them down, but they both stuck to their stories. I don't know why Tay should give her any money, but I'll take a bet he did. Well, what's he playing at?"

That I could work out with no difficulty. Why Daphne needed money and how Tay had learned this, I did not know. But his deal with her, I imagined, was the same as with me: he wanted her problematical votes. Andrew's story shook me, however, for that plus my own conversation with Tay had shown me how far he was willing to go to get control of the business. Perhaps he had been willing, as Andrew said, to go much further.

"I don't know what he's playing at," I said. "I gather Daphne is in trouble of some sort—that's probably why she went to talk to Uncle Hugh."

"Yes," said Andrew. "I've tried to get her to talk to me about it, but she won't. I'd help her if I could—but she knows that."

"What did Robert say?"

"He's very angry, of course. He still believes Daphne got the money from Uncle Hugh. He wants to know why she had to go to Uncle Hugh for money in the first place—what she was up to she didn't want him to know. But Daphne won't talk. You know how stubborn she can get. I know my sister isn't a murderer—but I wish she'd stop giving Burgess reasons for being suspicious."

VII

Directly after lunch—a strained meal, with Robert and Daphne pointedly ignoring each other—I went up to my room. I attended to a few small matters, and was about to go downstairs when I remembered that I had wanted to make a telephone call to the village. I picked up the receiver and heard a voice—Charles'—on the line.

I don't remember that I had ever before eavesdropped on anyone's conversation. But the whole situation was so abnormal that I, like everyone else, seemed to have departed from the ordinary canons of behaviour. Charles only said a few words, and then the voice at the other end of the wire said, "I appreciate your difficulties, old boy. But it's difficult for us, too. You left right in the middle of everything, you know—and the thing's at a standstill. I know you wanted to catch that plane, but it's certainly snarled things here."

Charles said with finality, "I'll call you again when I know what's happening," and hung up. So did I. So Charles had not, as he airily told us, finished "earlier than I had expected and caught a late plane". He had apparently left in the middle of some involved work and put his colleagues to considerable inconvenience. It was unlike Charles, who was very conscientious over his work. He must have had a very strong reason for wanting to be back that night. "I wanted to keep my father from making a public statement of his intentions." But surely Uncle Hugh wouldn't have done that before lunch? If Charles had caught the early plane in the morning, he would have had time enough to talk to Uncle Hugh before lunch.

I was still standing there staring stupidly at the telephone and trying not to reach any of the obvious conclusions when Mrs. Rapp knocked on the door and came in. Her opening remark was unpromising. "I'm not one to make trouble, as you know, Miss Christy," she began. "But I know my job. And I can't get on with it when people interfere at every turn with unwanted advice. It unsettles the staff as well—as if they weren't upset enough about poor Sir Hugh."

I agreed that my uncle's death must have been a great shock to the staff and more so to her; and added cautiously that everyone else was a bit upset, too. It was not to be that easy, however.

"If it was Mr. Charles that was making the trouble, well, that wouldn't be so bad. After all, Sir Hugh was his father, and it would be only right that he left Feathers to him. I'm sure no one would mind that. But to have that woman snooping and giving orders and her not even a relative—acting as if she was mistress here!—well, it's past bearing. Miss Christy I do wish you'd settle something or I can't answer for the staff. It's fortunate they haven't given notice already, but they'll be doing it soon if this goes on much longer."

"It's all very difficult," I agreed. I could well imagine what they had had to put up with from my aunt, and I did not envy them. "The trouble is, you see, things are very indefinite. When we know a bit more——" I stopped that sentence and started another one. "It's only a few days, Mrs. Rapp, till it'll all be settled. I could speak to Mr. Charles, but do you think you could keep things steady and take very little notice—for just a little longer?"

She did not reply right away. "I don't like to add to your troubles, Miss Chris," she said finally. "But if you'll forgive me saying so, you're still in charge here—until Sir Hugh's will is read, I mean. You could talk to your aunt, maybe—though it's not my place to give you any suggestions, I know."

She was perfectly right, of course; and too polite to say straight out that it was my responsibility rather than Charles'. I knew that; but the thought of coping with my aunt seemed more than I could manage at that point. "I'll see what I can do," I said. "But try not to take too much notice, if you can."

I don't know what her answer would have been; but there was again a knock on the door and Robert came in. Mrs. Rapp excused herself and went out, and I braced myself to deal with him. He said, "So I finally tracked you down, Chris. Tell me, has everyone in this house gone mad?"

I asked what he meant.

"You heard what happened this morning—about Daphne and the money, I mean?"

I said that I had.

"And then there's Daphne going in to see Uncle Hugh—why shouldn't she?—why such a mystery?—and letting it be dragged out of her by that little worm, Gresham. I swear, Chris, I wouldn't blame Burgess if he thought *she* had murdered Uncle Hugh. I don't, of course. She hadn't any reason to, and she wouldn't, anyway. But she needed money for something, and it can't be anything very savoury or she would have asked me for it. We're not short of money."

He stopped, and I said nothing. There was nothing to say. He was quite right on all counts. "And Andrew accusing Tay of giving her the money and Tay denying it. And everyone going around looking like death—including you. It isn't just that they're sorry about Uncle Hugh. That would be normal. But it looks to me as if you all suspect everyone else in the house of being a murderer!"

This was so close to my own feeling at the moment that I winced. But Robert was not noticing. "Well, Chris—why don't you say something?"

"There's nothing to say," I said. "I know we're all behaving abnormally. But———"

Robert interrupted me. "Do you know why Daphne needed the money?"

I said, "No. And I wouldn't tell you if I did. That's for her to tell you—if she wants to. But, Robert—I know you're right, of course—but could you possibly *not* ask her? Let it go, I mean. She's obviously distressed about something and she doesn't want to talk about it. Must you know?"

He considered this unreasonable, and I could not blame him. "If my wife becomes involved in something that makes her need money so badly she'll ask her uncle for it and not me—when I have enough—don't you think I should be concerned?"

"Oh, of course," I said, wearily. I wondered if it would help Daphne or Robert if I explained things—if I told him what it had been like for Daphne to grow up under the lynx-eyed watchfulness, social snobbery, and distorted values of my aunt and uncle. But, like everything else, it seemed too difficult, and I could not cope with it. Robert waited for me to say something else, but I didn't. We went downstairs together without speaking.

I spent most of the afternoon working with Charles on various practical details: a statement to be released to the newspapers; arrangements about the funeral on Wednesday morning and for the will to be read. Uncle Hugh's solicitor, Edward Temple, was coming down on Wednesday and would read the will that afternoon, after lunch.

We went over the newspaper statement carefully. It was a difficult thing to write, and no amount of caution or tact could make it sound good. "We're going to have trouble with reporters," I said. "We'd better make some arrangements so they don't get into the grounds."

"They'll pick most of it up in village gossip, I suppose," said Charles. "Well, it can't be helped. I wonder what they'll pick up in Redcot—I gather Giles is staying down there, or he was, over the week-end."

I made a non-committal reply, and Charles looked at me closely. "You're looking terrible, Christy—and it's not just my father's death. You look as if you had the weight of the world on your shoulders. What's the matter—concealing evidence?"

Something must have shown in my face at this, and Charles was much more observant than Robert. "Yes. I thought so. I'll take a guess that you know why Daphne needed money and who owns that lost cigarette-holder—not to mention various other details that have escaped Burgess. Why don't you tell him?"

"Tell him what?"

"Anything," said Charles, evenly. "Anything at all that you know. If I gather correctly from your tone that you think you know something discreditable to me, include that. Christy, let me remind you that my father was murdered. We may all get an unpleasant shock when we find out who did it, but it'll be much better than never knowing at all. Besides, it's very bad for anyone to get away with a murder successfully. They might be encouraged and try it again."

"You may be right," I said. I felt very nearly at the end of my tether. "But I'm willing to leave it up to Burgess. I just don't want to be involved in it at all."

"Or in anything," said my cousin. "At least, I presume that's why you let Aunt Mildred drive Mrs. Rapp practically to the point of leaving, when the house is really your responsibility. But what are you afraid of, Chris? Doing something wrong? It'd be much better than brooding and doing nothing at all. Burgess is no fool, you know. If I can tell you're concealing information, so can he. He's probably looking for it."

I did not answer. Charles said, more gently, "You're getting it out of focus, Chris. We're not all murderers—just one of us is. And he—or she—will be discovered. The world won't come to an end, any more than it did when my father was killed. But you mustn't get into your head the idea that because one of us murdered him, any one of us is capable of murder. It's just not true, my dear. Don't you trust anyone?"

I wanted to say no: no one—and, least of all, myself. I did not. Charles said, his voice more gentle still, "One mistake doesn't invalidate your judgment—and shouldn't paralyse you for life, Christy."

I still said nothing, and we sat in silence. It had become dim in the room, and neither of us had troubled to put on the light. For a few moments, I relaxed in the first comfort I had known since my uncle had been killed. I thought Charles had taken considerable thought and trouble over me, more than I would have expected him to do. But the possibility of his being a murderer remained.

I faced it coldly. Did I actually believe he had killed his father?

It was far from impossible. He had the three classic requirements: means, motive, and opportunity. For all that my Aunt Mildred might say, Charles was his father's son. His father gave him what I suppose was a generous allowance; but it was nothing to what my cousin might expect now Uncle Hugh was dead. Charles had always, from an early age, said he would not go into the business. But it was bigger now than it had ever been, and the man who controlled it had a great deal of power. Who was to say what Charles might not be able to do, with his father out of the way? It was unlikely that he would be able to control the company by himself; but, by throwing his support to one or another faction, he might get a good deal for himself. This might be pure fantasy, as I did not think Charles, any more than anyone else, knew the contents of his father's will. I did not think so; but I did not know. So whether he wanted financial independence or some voice in the business, Charles—from some points of view—had good reason to want his father dead.

The answer to it all was simple: I did not know who had killed my uncle. But it could be Charles as easily as anyone else—and more easily than some of the other possible suspects. Rational analysis made that clear enough; and it was clear that my venture into other fields had not been significantly successful.

Charles took out a cigarette and gave me one, too. He leaned forward and switched on the light. At that moment, Burgess came into the library. Charles showed him the Press release, and Burgess said he thought it would do quite well. "My men might be able to give you some help in keeping reporters at a reasonable distance."

We talked about Wednesday's arrangements for a few minutes, after which Charles asked Burgess if he wanted a whisky. Burgess said yes, and added that he had wanted a word with Charles in any case and this was a convenient place and time. I asked if I should go.

"No," said Burgess. "I'd rather you stayed."

Uncle Hugh always kept a bottle of whisky and some glasses in the wall-cupboard. Charles poured us each a drink, sat down again, and looked at Burgess.

Burgess took a swallow of his whisky and said it was very good. "It's about that call from Paris, Mr. Mason. You had one this afternoon, I think."

"Yes."

"I gathered from your conversation that you'd left in a hurry, leaving a lot of work not only unfinished but badly tied up. Yet you told me yesterday you'd come back earlier than you'd intended because you'd finished your work. The two statements don't go together very well, do they? Perhaps you'd like to explain."

"They don't, that's true," said Charles. He was, as far as I could tell, entirely unruffled. "The truth is that I decided to come back in a hurry and I left some reasonably important things rather in the air. I didn't come back with any murderous intentions, however. I'd heard some rather alarming things—at least, I considered them alarming— about my father's plans for the Freemen. They bothered me, and I found I wasn't concentrating on my work. So I decided to come back and find out for myself."

"I see," said Burgess, politely. "I take it you succeeded in finding out everything you needed to know in the twenty-minute conversation you had with your father on Saturday night."

"I found it out in ten minutes," said Charles. "It took me five to learn what his plans were, and another five to learn that he wasn't planning to be swayed. Maybe less."

The two regarded each other for a moment. "It's not the most plausible story I've ever heard," remarked Burgess.

Charles smiled. "I could think of a more plausible one easily. But this one happens to be true."

"Very well. Are there any other corrections you'd like to make to your story?"

"Not corrections," said Charles. "Everything else I told you was the truth. But I'd like to make an addition. I don't know that it'll be very helpful, since it just confirms what you already know. My father did say to me, 'This seems to be my evening for callers. I've had two already.' From what was said yesterday, that would have been Uncle William and Tay."

"Probably," said Burgess. "You've just remembered this?"

"That's right."

Burgess regarded my cousin in a speculative manner. He did not say he did not believe Charles' story. But I guessed that he was thinking just what I had thought: if anyone had the coolness required to commit a murder and get away with it, Charles had. I think Charles himself understood what was in our minds, but he only smiled amiably and poured us each another drink. Then he said to Burgess, and his eyes were mocking, "You know, I could almost find it in my heart to feel sorry for your murderer. You've tied him up very tight."

Burgess' eyes were as ironic as Charles' own. "I have?"

My cousin was clearly enjoying himself. "You have. In fact, looked at from his own point of view, the murderer's had damn bad luck. He's had literally no time at all to clean up after himself—or herself, of course," he added. "He leaves the drug in my father's carafe and goes away. He has no time to check up on anything—to see that he's left no loose ends. Instead, the maid finds the body early in the morning, everyone is penned up in the library, and Gresham makes his accusations and gets the Yard called in straightaway. You bring all your men in with you and we've all been under constant surveillance. If he had left any loose ends, it's just too bad for him."

Burgess did not by so much as a flicker of the eyelids offer a clue to what he was thinking. "Are you suggesting the Yard wouldn't have been called in if Gresham hadn't been here?"

"I'm not sure. I think you probably would have been—only not so soon. And I should think a murderer needs time. You have to be very clever and very lucky to get away with murder. But you also have to be very thorough. This was obviously a quick job—and there's been no time for thoroughness."

"You appear to have given the matter a great deal of thought."

"Yes," said my cousin. "You see, it happened to my father—and among my relatives. So I've been spending the last few days thinking about it—the last two, I mean. Seems longer, somehow."

"And have you worked out," asked Burgess, "what slip the murderer could have made? Or, if you prefer, what he had to tie up?" His tone was cold and expressionless. I felt very chilly and very much alone. They were clearly conducting some kind of battle of wits, and had forgotten me for the moment. I could not make out what Charles was doing: whether he was coldly taunting Burgess, telling him to find some evidence that he, Charles, was the murderer—if he could; or whether he was trying obliquely to give Burgess some information which he was for some reason unwilling to give openly and plainly.

"I can think of only one thing," said my cousin, slowly. "I don't think there's a way around just one piece of evidence—one that couldn't be explained away, I mean. But, of course"—he deliberately broke the mood—"it's nothing I know much about."

The tension dropped by a good many points, and Burgess smiled at me. "Your cousin might make a good detective, Mrs. Fane."

"Only fair," said Charles. "I can't find out why Christy was wandering about this morning, for instance—or where she went."

I started to say he had not asked me, and stopped. Burgess said, "I can tell you that. She went to Redcot, to call on her cousin, Giles. Why she went there is another matter. I could ask her, of course, but I'm not entirely sure I'll get a truthful answer."

"Now there," said Charles, "I agree with you. She'll probably say she just went to talk about old times and assorted subjects. And I don't suppose you could prove otherwise."

"I couldn't," said Burgess. "But, like you, I wouldn't care for the story. Somehow, I don't think anyone would rush down in that way to see a cousin like Giles Randall under these circumstances unless there was a pressing motive. Care to tell me what it was, Mrs. Fane?"

"I went," I said, clearly, "to talk about old times and assorted subjects."

Burgess got up. "All right," he said. "I'll find out soon anyway, you know. By the way, Mrs. Fane, don't go for any more walks on your own, will you? Just till we get this thing cleared up."

Left alone, Charles and I regarded each other with some interest. "He will, you know," said Charles. "He's brainy enough. Christy, what on earth are you playing at?"

"That's just what I was going to ask you," I said.

Burgess dined with us that night. Later, while we were having coffee, I saw him talking to Andrew and Tay in one corner of the room. Anne and Daphne were sitting together on a sofa, somewhat removed from the rest of us, and conversing in low tones. I heard Andrew give an exclamation and then say something urgently to Tay. Tay shrugged his shoulders and Burgess nodded. He said, addressing all of us, "I've been telling Mr. Mason and Mr. Tay one or two of the things we've learned so far. Some matters take longer than others to check. But I see no objection to telling all of you the results of our investigations in one field—to date."

Daphne and Anne stopped talking abruptly and I stopped my desultory chat with Robert. Charles, who had been politely resisting all my aunt's revisions of Wednesday's programme, turned sharply and looked at Tay, Andrew and Burgess. Burgess said, "It has to do with what I had considered to be two previous attempts on Sir Hugh's life."

In a moment, any warmth in the room had disappeared. In its place were shock—and fear. But no one said anything. Burgess went on smoothly, "I refer, of course, to the motor-car accident in which

Sir Hugh, Mrs. Fane, and the chauffeur, Raikes, were involved; and to an illness which Sir Hugh had, following the taking of a digestive pill, in Birmingham. You all knew about the accident, I believe, though perhaps none of you considered that it might have been an attempt at murder. I think only you, Mrs. Fane, knew about Sir Hugh's indisposition in Birmingham."

Everyone stared at me. The faces looked unfriendly. My Aunt Mildred said, frostily, "Really, Chris, you might have mentioned it to someone."

"Raikes," said Burgess, "was concerned about the accident and thought it must have been deliberately caused. He made some investigations on his own and worked out a method by which he thought it might have been done. We are, of course, looking into it thoroughly. He did not know about the episode in Birmingham. Mrs. Fane, however, did suggest to Sir Hugh himself that these two accidents might have been contrived deliberately. Sir Hugh—not entirely to her surprise—made light of it."

"Chris," said Andrew, "you must have known he wouldn't take it seriously. Why didn't you talk to one of us about it? We might even have prevented what happened."

"As it happens," said Burgess, before I could reply, "I now have decided that the illness in Birmingham was just that, and not an attempt at murder. I spoke to the doctor in Birmingham and your London doctor, Barker, did, too. Barker assures me that Sir Hugh's symptoms were merely those of a serious digestive upset. He does not think any other conclusions reasonable—and I now agree with him. I should add"—he surveyed us in a leisurely manner—"that Dr. Barker confirmed the fact that he had a large stock of hexamethonium bromide on hand. He doesn't keep a very careful check on it. So it would be quite easy for anyone to remove some of his supply without his noticing it."

No one missed the implications of that. Burgess said, "Well, I think that's all I have to say."

"But you didn't answer Andrew's question, Chris," said my Uncle William. "If you knew all this, why didn't you say something to one of us?"

I said, "Well, I wasn't sure that——" But Charles interrupted me. He had not missed the motive Burgess had in appearing to give out information so freely. Burgess obviously wanted to rattle all of us, especially the murderer, and to set us all against each other. (I rather thought the latter was unnecessary.) Charles, for his own reasons, decided to help. "Chris was in a delicate position," he said. "You remember there was a family dinner the night before the three of them left for Birmingham. So she reasoned that any one of us could have tampered with the tyre."

If my family's faces had looked unfriendly before, they now showed positive dislike. Uncle William said, "Chris—did you really think that one of us—tampered with Hugh's car? You must have been mad."

"Of course, one of us seems to have murdered him with hexamethonium bromide," said Charles. "I don't see why tampering with a car comes into a different category."

Everyone started to talk at once. I don't know what might have been said, but Tay got the floor. "May I ask a question, Inspector? I understood you to say that you were investigating the car smash. But surely there's very little left to investigate. Presumably, the old tyre has long since been sent to scrap—if there was enough of it left even for that. I should imagine it would be impossible to trace. So I don't see what further investigation could be expected to reveal."

The Inspector had too much self-control to show the annoyance he must have felt. Everyone—with the possible exception of Aunt Mildred—grasped Tay's point, and there was a noticeable easing of tension. Others besides myself must have grasped the point Tay did not make aloud: that even if Burgess could work out exactly how the tyre had been tampered with, all proof had been destroyed. I wondered who or what Tay had been trying to save or to protect by his well-timed intervention. I am sure Burgess wondered, too.

General conversation more or less ceased after that. Tay's intervention had lowered the general tension, but had not eliminated it. Charles' comments on my reluctance to trust any of my relatives plus Burgess' evident certainty that he would sooner or later unmask the murderer among us had again brought us all up against the facts which we tried to evade. This was an investigation for murder; and no amount of tactful behaviour by the police, comfort in physical surroundings, and an attempt at normal behaviour could in the end disguise it. I was again overcome by the feeling of apprehension I had been fighting all day, and the others must have felt the same. We were all acutely uncomfortable in each other's company, and everyone went to bed early.

Anne came up with me, and stopped by for a cigarette in my room. She sat there in an arm-chair, looking very calm and normal. I thought she was the only one of us who seemed unaffected by the tension of the past two days; yet on Saturday at lunch I had thought for a moment that she looked a bit strained. She said, "That was quite a scene, wasn't it? I imagine Burgess was annoyed."

"I suppose so."

"He seems very thorough, of course. I don't think he'll stop trying to find out who tampered with the car—if anyone did—just because he wouldn't get a case that would stand up in court. He probably thinks that if he's certain who did wreck the tyre, it'll make it much easier for him to solve this case—assuming the same person made both attempts."

"Probably." It did not sound so serious when she spoke of it—more like a problem in chess than a murder investigation.

Anne changed the subject. "You know, Daphne's behaving very oddly."

I agreed.

"You don't think she's unbalanced enough to commit a murder, do you?"

She asked the question as easily as if she had asked me to pass the marmalade. "I shouldn't have thought so," I said, wearily, "though I'll admit I'm not sure of anything at the moment."

Anne ignored the second half of my sentence. "I don't know why she wanted money or who gave it to her or why she went in to see Uncle Hugh. But I do know that with murder involved, it's foolish of her not to tell the truth—and get suspected of something worse than the mess she's probably in."

"Who suspects her?"

"The policeman, for one. He suspects everyone. And I, for another."

"You? You can't possibly."

"She's behaving very oddly," said Anne again. "And I've never thought her very stable. She clearly hasn't got much common sense. If she hasn't done the murder and is making Burgess suspicious of her, it's surely very unwise. Besides, she hasn't got much point to her life, has she? If she breaks up her marriage, she'll have none at all. Yet she seems to be going out of her way to do it. Robert suspects all kinds of things, and he'll make it his business to find out. If it is something like that, she'd be far wiser to tell him herself. On the other hand, if she did do the murder, she's certainly going about things in a very stupid way—not admitting she'd been to see Uncle Hugh, getting excited about being caught with the money—everything."

It was a long speech for Anne, who was normally not very talkative. I looked at her with respect. "You're less upset by this murder than anyone else. Of course, he wasn't really your uncle—I realize that. But I don't believe you care whether the murderer gets caught or not."

"I don't. I'm sorry about the murder, of course. I liked your uncle. But since he *is* dead, I can't see what end would be served by finding the murderer. It would only mean unpleasant publicity—and we're going to have enough of that as it is."

"Well, it's a point of view," I said. "And it's cool enough."

Anne smiled. "It's also sensible. I'm a realist, Chris, not a romantic. You get that way if you come from a family that's been rich and influential for a long time."

She paused to light a cigarette. I said, half jokingly, "Have you had any murders in your family?"

"Not recently. But there were some dubious episodes early on. Any old family has a lot of blots in its collective copy-book. They don't matter, Chris—any more than some of the things your uncle must have done in building up his fortune matter. Well, I'm now going to bed. But, Christy—see if you can talk a little sense to Daphne. Maybe she'll listen to you."

I said that I would try, and Anne went off. I remained sitting in front of the fire, thinking. I was not especially surprised by Anne's remarks; they were entirely in character. She was an ideal wife for Andrew, I reflected. They agreed on so many things—chiefly on being unsentimental. I imagined that she and Andrew had agreed entirely on the affair of Apex Springs. I wondered whether Burgess knew about that business—or what he would think of it if he did.

There was a small company in the north of England called Apex Springs Limited. It belonged to some people called Larkin, and had been in the family for three generations. For about twenty years Apex had supplied Uncle Hugh's business with a particular kind of spring. Originally, they had had a large number of customers, but gradually they came to sell most of these special springs—by far the largest part of their output—to Uncle Hugh's firm. In the years after the war, these springs came to be more in demand, and Andrew, whose responsibility this was, decided to arrange for Uncle Hugh's firm to manufacture the springs itself. This, after some manœuvring, he did.

It was not until his new arrangements were complete that Andrew told Larkin about them. Their contracts were subject to cancellation with three months' notice on either side; and Andrew correctly gave this notice. This sudden action naturally meant great difficulties for Apex Springs and even included the possibility of bankruptcy. When pressed by Larkin, however, to put off cancelling his contracts for a year, or at least to continue to buy small quantities while the firm rebuilt its buyers' list, Andrew refused. He did not do so out of any especial coldness or dislike for Larkin. In fact, if anything, he probably rather liked the man. But his arrangements had been very precisely made, and he intended to have them stand. They did stand.

Andrew at no time saw anything at all unusual in what he had done. If he *had* informed the man of his intentions in advance, Larkin would quite naturally have started looking for other customers immediately and no doubt supplying them. This might have inconvenienced Uncle Hugh's firm and this, Andrew, who liked efficiency, would not have. Andrew was not unaware of the difficulties Larkin and the Apex Company would face. He simply did not recognize that it had anything to do with him.

"Andrew will go a long way," Charles had said, in speaking of the episode. "I'm afraid Tay might see the other side's case against him, even if he did nothing about it. Andrew's great strength is that he doesn't see it."

"Would you have done it?" I asked.

"The question doesn't arise," Charles had said. "I'm not in the business—nor likely to be. But that's the kind of man who'll stay afloat when his rivals go down. It's a point worth remembering."

Even at the time, I had wondered if Charles was being quite candid, or whether his attitude had concealed a certain admiration not unmixed with envy. I know that now I envied both Andrew and Anne one thing: they were realists. Some might think that this made them logical suspects as murderers. But I did not think this necessarily true. There was this to be said for a realistic approach to life: if you had it, you acted. You did not dither around, never taking any decisive action until it was too late, and thus allow yourself to be pushed into a situation where you had to take desperate measures.

I realized that the fire had gone out and that I was cold. I threw my cigarette into the grate and went to bed.

VIII

I slept very late Tuesday morning. It was probably the combination of sleeping-pills and exhaustion. I did not come down to breakfast until 10.30. While I was having my coffee, Charles came in. "You're very late," he observed. "Just as well, too—you've missed all the reporters."

"You've got rid of them?"

"With some difficulty. I think they're picking up what they can in the village and they'll turn up outside the church to-morrow. But we're safe for the rest of to-day, I think. Oh—by the way—we've a new arrival at the house."

"A new arrival? Who?"

"Giles."

I stiffened. "What's he doing here?"

"He came by request—and under escort. Burgess found out that the amber cigarette-holder is his, as I've no doubt you knew all the time. Since the maid found it early Sunday morning and an observant bartender at the village pub saw Giles use it Saturday night, an explanation seems indicated. Burgess is talking to him in the sitting-room now."

At this moment, Mrs. Rapp came into the dining-room. From the look on her face, it was not hard to guess that she had had more trouble with my aunt. Before she could say anything, however, a young police-sergeant who was working with Burgess came in. "The Inspector would like to see you in the sitting-room, Mrs. Fane, when you've finished your breakfast," he said, "if you don't mind."

"I'll come now," I said. "May I see you later, Mrs. Rapp?"

Giles looked shockingly bad, tired and pale, with circles under his eyes. He said hello curtly when I came in, and nothing more. Burgess looked almost ostentatiously patient.

"I've been trying to persuade Mr. Randall to make a statement," he told me. "But he's refused flatly to say anything. His cigarette-holder, which was last in his possession at about 10.30 Saturday night, was found here early Sunday morning. It was quite easy for anyone to get into this house unnoticed. Your cousin, Mr. Charles Mason, managed it, with no trouble. Mr. Randall's relations with his uncle are quite well known. In spite of all this, he persists in saying that he was not in the house and that he does not wish to say anything else. I sent for you in the hope that you might influence him to use a little common sense."

Burgess was clearly talking to Giles, though he was ostensibly speaking to me. The case he had against Giles was his most promising one to date. Burgess was, I thought, a very fair man, but I imagined that Giles' mulish silence must be yet another point in the case against himself. I had little hope of influencing my cousin, but I tried.

"Giles," I said, "Inspector Burgess has been here two days. He seems very reasonable. He's no more prejudiced against you than against the rest of us. But he's bound to come to the worst possible conclusion if you refuse to say anything."

"This doesn't concern you, Chris," said Giles. "You manage your own affairs and I'll take care of mine."

"You don't seem to be doing it very successfully at the moment. The only thing sillier than getting arrested for a murder you did commit would be to get arrested for one you didn't."

Burgess listened to this cynical remark without noticeable emotion. So did Giles, who said nothing. "Well," I said to Burgess, "I'm not doing any good here. Why don't you get Charles in? He's the only one Giles might conceivably listen to. You needn't bother with any of the others."

"There is no need to bring in Charles," said Giles, annoyed. "I'm not a difficult child who has to be coaxed and I rely on my own judgment to tell me what to say or what not to say."

"He's always had bad judgment, of course," I said to Burgess. "Funny how far back it goes. He couldn't judge our nurse's temper in the nursery. Runs right through everything he does—even driving. I remember once, years ago, we drove into Redcot for something. There was a van parked on the side of the road. Giles cut around it and another car was coming the other way. Instead of speeding up, he executed some fancy manœuvre and we ended up in the ditch."

"I executed no fancy manœuvre," said Giles. "I did the only thing that could save us from being killed—and I did save us, you notice. You know, Inspector, Christy's told that story for years and it's never been correct. But she goes right on telling it." He glared at me with such frustrated anger that one would have thought the accident had just taken place. The Inspector looked from one of us to the other and began to laugh; so did I, and so—finally—did Giles.

When we had stopped laughing, there was silence for a moment, and then Giles said, "Oh—the devil with it, Christy—I suppose there's no way out." He turned to the Inspector. "If I make a statement, will I be free to go?"

Burgess shook his head. "I can't say that, Mr. Randall. If you make a statement, we'll naturally check as much of it as we can. But since you were in the house that night, I'd prefer you to stay here with the others, if Mrs. Fane can arrange it. It saves having to keep a man watching you down in the village, you see."

"It'll be just like old times to have him staying here," I said, politely. "I'll try to give you the room next to Uncle William and Aunt Mildred."

"Oh, hell," said Giles. "All right. What do you want to know, Inspector?"

"The whole story—what time you came here and why. What you said to your uncle. When you left."

"Well," said my cousin, "I can't tell you exactly when I came, but it must have been one o'clock or a bit later. I walked over from Redcot…"

Giles had found Uncle Hugh working at his desk. He was wearing a silk dressing-gown over his shirt and trousers, and he looked opulent and at ease with himself. He must have been surprised to see Giles, but he showed no signs of it. Nor did he appear either curious or annoyed. "Good evening, Giles. I can't say I expected you, but I'd heard you'd been in these parts a bit lately."

"From your sister-in-law and the servants, no doubt."

"Well," said my uncle, mildly, "they've all seen you grow up. It's not surprising they should take an interest in your activities."

"I've not come to talk about that, in any case," said my cousin, shortly. "I've come to talk to you—and about you."

My uncle raised his eyebrows slightly. "Then sit down, my boy—unless you're planning to give a lecture."

Giles remained standing. "It won't take long. I've come to tell you I know all about your activities in that Fascist organization, the Freemen of Britain."

"That's not surprising, considering the interest you've always taken in my affairs. What about it?"

Giles had been slightly taken aback. He had expected a different reaction: annoyance, concern, alarm; not this unaffected calm. He said, "I've come to tell you that unless you withdraw all your support from them completely, I'll make your activities known to everyone in Britain."

"You must please yourself, of course, Giles. But there's no need for you to go to all that trouble. I shall be making a public announcement of it myself in any case—in a speech on Wednesday night."

Giles was no fool. He had known my uncle for many years, and he knew that he had been told the truth. He realized that he had miscalculated. He had been certain that my uncle planned to remain entirely anonymous and in the background of the Freemen. But Uncle Hugh's calm statement made it clear that the organization was going to make an open bid for political power. Giles could not interpret it in any other way. He said, "You know it's a bloody Fascist organization."

"We needn't quarrel about terms. I know quite well what the organization is, yes. I've been influential in its development, so I ought to know."

"And to keep your miserable money, you'd establish a tyranny over the people of this country—oh, a decent, well-bred tyranny, I don't doubt, but dictatorship just the same. Well, it won't work, you know. You won't get away with it. The workers of this country are on to people like you."

"Well, if you're right," said my uncle, equably, "you've nothing to worry about, have you? But you're a bit confused, my dear boy. I've made my money honestly and I'd like to keep it. You're right there. But I'm reasonably attached to the old ways—parliament, democracy, and all that—for whatever they're worth. The point is that the system's not working any more—not efficiently, that is. When that happens, another system takes its place. My own belief is that the new system will be some form of dictatorship. Everything's moving that way. Well, it'll be a dictatorship of the Left, if you have your way. You'd have one to-day, if you thought you could get away with it. If I have my way, it'll be a dictatorship of the Right—which will be much more suitable for England in any case."

"And you think you'll get away with it? You think the working people of this country will stand for it?"

"I think so," said my uncle. He was entirely calm and dispassionate. "I understand ordinary people better than you do. I'm afraid being an intellectual and an old Etonian is a fatal handicap when it comes to understanding ordinary people. The trouble with you—and with some of your friends—is that they think working people are either like them or that they ought to be. You want to improve them. One of your complaints against my lot is that we don't want to improve the workers. But if they don't want to be improved, that's our strength, not our weakness."

Giles' violent anger did not keep him from speaking. "You're very plausible," he said, bitterly. "You're very plausible. You'll offer them bread and circuses and all you'll ask will be their freedom. You'll trick them into giving up what they've struggled for and make them grateful to you for thinking for them. Is that it?"

"You ought to know," said my uncle, amiably. "The prescription's that of your friends, isn't it? Give them what's good for them, whether they like it or not. You'll tell me you're doing it to ensure the welfare of the people and that we'll only do it for power. But who's to say you're right? Who's to say people won't be better-governed and happier under what you're pleased to call a tyranny of the Right than under what I call a tyranny of the Left? And who's to say what the motives of either of us *really* are? I say I want efficiency and you say you want the welfare of the people. But my enemies will no doubt say I want power—and your enemies will say the same about you. And who's to judge where the truth lies?"

"I've always hated you," said Giles. "All my life. But I don't think I ever realized how wicked you were. It's an old-fashioned word—wicked. But then, you're an old-fashioned man, aren't you? Well, I hoped to make you see some reason to-night, but I know the impossible when I come across it. Let me tell you just one thing, though—to make it clear. I'll fight your organization with every weapon I have. But if I ever come to think you're so important to it that your death would harm it, I'll kill you myself! And I mean that. Don't forget it!"

He left the room, then. He caught just the end of my uncle's amused remark. It was something to the effect that surely Eton should have concentrated more on developing poise and self-control...

When Giles had finished, I was sick with apprehension. I was angry, too. It was just like Giles, I thought. He had never had any judgment and when he was talking about my uncle, he had no self-control. That he had sneaked into the house was bad enough. That he had not come forward with this information when he learned my uncle had been murdered could be considered misguided, if no worse. His account of the earlier part of the interview showed clearly that his temper had been very high. But for him to recount that last part and his final words was sheer lunacy. It was like asking for a conviction of murder.

And yet, looking at the Inspector, I wondered if I were right. It could be argued the other way: a guilty man would not have admitted making such a threat. Perhaps the very ugliness of Giles' story made it more likely to be true. Well, the men in my family in this generation were at least alike, I thought—Giles, Andrew, and Charles, each presenting to the Inspector all the damning facts about themselves, and daring him to see what he could make of them.

Burgess heard Giles' rather incriminating story with polite impassivity. He then asked the sergeant, who had been taking shorthand notes, whether he had got the story straight. The sergeant, less impassive than his superior, nodded. He looked appalled.

Giles seemed to come to himself suddenly. He looked at the sergeant, at the note-book in which his words had been recorded, and at Burgess. For a moment, I thought he seemed alarmed and was going to protest. But he didn't. He had many faults, but he did not lack courage. I wondered if the Inspector knew Giles had been a Commando during the war.

"Is that all?" asked my cousin.

"A few more points, if you don't mind, Mr. Randall. You say you arrived here shortly after one in the morning. How long were you here altogether?"

"I should think—oh, twenty minutes, perhaps. Twenty-five at the outside."

"What kind of spirits was your uncle in? I mean, did he seem depressed? Did you have any reason to think he might be contemplating suicide?"

Giles laughed. "Uncle Hugh kill himself? The last man in the world! He was much too pleased with himself!"

"Then you would say he seemed much as usual?"

"He certainly talked just as usual. I thought he seemed a little quieter and more subdued than normal, and he said once or twice that it was cold in his room. Actually, it was rather warm."

"Did he say he felt ill?"

"He wasn't ill," said Giles, impatiently. "And he didn't say so. I imagine he was tired. It was late at night, you know."

All right, said Burgess. "Tell me, Mr. Randall, when did you learn that your uncle had been killed?"

"Sunday morning. One of the village girls told Miss Moore, and she told me."

"Did you learn how he had been killed?"

"No. I don't actually know yet, though I heard it was some form of poison."

"Not precisely," said Burgess. "Your uncle was given a large dose of hexamethonium bromide in his water carafe. It's rather a new drug. Have you ever heard of it?"

Giles answered almost immediately—but not quite; there was a barely perceptible pause. "I think I have."

"Do you know what its effects are?"

"It's something to do with lowering the blood pressure, isn't it? I think I've read about it."

"Yes," said Burgess. "Well, that's all for now, Mr. Randall. I may want to talk to you again later. You can ring Mrss Moore's cottage now, if you like, and tell her any things you may want up here. One of my men will go down for them later on."

"I'm under protective custody?" asked Giles, sarcastically.

"No more than anyone else," said Burgess, evenly.

Giles gave it up and went out, presumably to telephone. Burgess said to me. "You don't have to answer this question, Mrs. Fane, but I'd like to know: is your cousin a Communist?"

I said, "Are you interested in politics?"

"Yes."

"And—this will sound rude, but I don't mean it that way—do you know anything about it?"

"Yes."

"Then," I said, "no. Giles is not a Communist."

Burgess smiled. "For the simpler minded, he is?"

I smiled, too. "He isn't really, of course. He's certainly never received any Moscow gold, and I'm sure he's never been a member of the party. But since he always defends or excuses the Russians and as his general line is often similar to though not identical with theirs, ordinary people who don't take much interest in politics can't be blamed for getting confused."

"What *are* his political views, then? He doesn't entirely dislike the idea of dictatorship?"

I hesitated. "I don't suppose he actually favours it. But neither is he averse to it, should it be necessary—and he and his friends would be the sole judges of whether it was necessary or not. He's out to improve people and the way they live, and if they don't see the light, he's willing to do it by compulsion. He wouldn't put it exactly that way, of course. He'd say they'd been misled and corrupted by the rich—by which he means anyone who doesn't share his own political views, it has nothing to do with the income level, necessarily."

"That dislike for the class he came from—it can't *all* be because he hated Sir Hugh?"

"Oh, no—though that's an important part of it. But I grant you there are a lot of people who share Giles' general views without having a specific relative to hate. I've never really worked it out. But he and his friends are convinced that they are the only people who really mean well."

"Your family must be very upset at having a close relative with Mr. Randall's views."

"Most of them. Not all of them. I told you Uncle Hugh wasn't. Charles isn't. I'm not. Uncle William would dislike Giles' views just as badly if he were nothing more revolutionary than a peaceful follower of Mr. Attlee."

A policeman came in and handed an envelope to the Inspector. As Burgess read it, his face changed. He seemed to look older—and harder—and more worried. He said "Thanks", and the man left. Burgess continued to look at the message as if he could somehow extract from it more than was on the paper. I made a move to go, but he waved me back. "We were talking about Mr. Randall's political beliefs, weren't we?" He sounded a world away.

"Yes."

"You're sure? I mean, you'd bank on your analysis of how he'd behave?"

He sounded less incisive than usual. It was evident that the message—whatever it was—had upset him.

"I wouldn't put it just that way," I said. I could hardly have told him I'd bank on my analysis of nothing. "It's just—the impression I have of Giles."

Burgess seemed to take himself in hand. "You said 'he's certainly never received any Moscow gold.' You're at least sure of that? He wouldn't—well, for instance, he wouldn't give away secrets to the Russians?"

No one chooses an example like that at random. I knew Burgess, a careful man, had not. Perhaps he would not have used it at all if he had not been shocked by the note he'd just been given. I said, "No. I don't think so." And something stirred far back in my mind—something—I said, almost unconscious that I spoke aloud, "Secrets—has there been a leak from the lab at Uncle Hugh's plant?"

He jumped to it so sharply that I was startled. "What d'you know about it?"

"I don't." I was still speaking very slowly. This thing must have been at the back of my mind for some time, though I had not been aware of it. "You just said—would Giles sell secrets. And you'd had a note that disturbed you. I suppose I put two and two together—or maybe more. You see, on Saturday morning when I went into the library to ask if there was anything I could do, my uncle was just finishing a conversation on the telephone. I heard him say 'No. I've got it. I'll see to it immediately. Don't worry.' He looked angry—and a little queer. Then he saw me and spoke quite normally. So I forgot about it. After he was killed, I remembered it—but I thought it might have had something to do with the Freemen."

"You say he looked queer. What do you mean by queer—ill?"

"No." I searched for the right word. "Not ill at all. I don't know—outraged, perhaps. That's the closest I can come to it."

"Outraged," said Burgess. "Yes. I suppose that might be it. No, I don't think it has anything to do with the Freemen, Mrs. Fane. Your guess was quite right. I must ask you to give me your word you'll not repeat this conversation."

"You have it," I said.

"Very well. There *has* been some leakage at your uncle's plant. They only told him of it a short time ago—well, they only learned of it a short time ago, to be accurate. He said he'd look into it—they preferred it that way, too. He was talking to one of the Intelligence people Saturday morning—about eleven. Is that about when you went into the library?"

"About that," I said. I felt sick. Burgess and I looked at each other.

"I can imagine how you feel," he said. "It's not very pretty. It shakes you to think of something like—treason—coming so close, doesn't it?"

"It makes the world seem—even shakier than usual."

"Of course," said Burgess. "This sort of thing isn't exactly my line, but naturally I've come across it before. It still shakes me, in spite of some experience with it. And it's going to complicate this case badly. It seemed like an ordinary case of murder—with extraordinary people involved, perhaps. But now it's more complicated—and more urgent."

I said, "But surely you don't *know* it was someone here? And even if it was—my uncle might have been killed for a quite different reason?"

"I agree, Mrs. Fane. But it's a coincidence all the same. And I don't like coincidences like this. Still—there may be one case, there may be two. They'll have to be sorted out."

His voice was quite level. When I looked beyond it to what was meant by that neutral phrase "sorted out", I again felt sick and I could feel my hands begin to shake. Burgess said, "Shall I get you a drink?"

I shook my head. "I'm all right—or I will be in a minute."

He gave me a cigarette and took one himself. After a moment he said, "Did you know what kind of secret work they were doing at your uncle's plant?"

I shook my head. "I think everyone takes it for granted that plants like that do some secret research. And I knew there was a lab only certain people could enter. But that was all. Was the leakage about something—important?"

"All leakages are important. This isn't on the atom bomb level or anything near it, of course. But it's serious enough. Mrs. Fane, you say only certain people could go into one lab. Do you know who—or how many?"

"I've no idea. I should suppose the scientists and a few workmen, possibly, and some of the top administrative people. But it's only a guess."

"I'm guessing rather a lot myself at this point, Mrs. Fane, but good detective work—any detective work—depends a good deal on intuition. Has to. Something seems to fit or it doesn't. You don't know why and you're not always right. But you're right more often than you're wrong. It saves time and energy to investigate your hunches first—if they're as consistent with what happened as any other possibility. So— you said your uncle looked outraged. Do you think he was looking outraged at the general idea of a leakage at his plant?"

"Of course."

"I don't think so, Mrs. Fane. He certainly would have been outraged when he first heard about it. But he'd known for some days by the time you overheard him speaking to Intelligence. So it's much more likely that he was outraged at what he'd learned."

It sounded logical. I said so.

"And he'd be more outraged if the leak had something to do with his family than if anyone else had been involved, wouldn't he?"

I started to protest. Burgess forestalled me. "It's not proof," he said, wearily. "I know that. I'm just dealing with suppositions. Let me put it this way: he'd have been somewhat outraged if the leak had been through an ordinary workman, more so if it'd been through a scientist or one of the top administrative staff—and most outraged if it had been through a member of his own family."

There was no arguing with that. I again agreed.

"Then—let's put it at its bluntest, Mrs. Fane. Suppose your uncle had learned that one of the members of his family had been the cause of the leakage of information. He'd have taken some strong action just the same, wouldn't he? He wouldn't protect the person just because he was in the family?"

I shook my head. "I honestly don't know what he'd have done. He'd have tried to hush it up, of course—to see that nothing was made public. But he'd have taken—very drastic action just the same." I realized suddenly what we were saying and what was involved, and the shock of disbelief came over me again. I burst out, "It seems impossible."

Burgess' voice was not unsympathetic. "You mean it seems impossible that a member of your family could be a convinced Communist— or willing to give them information, for whatever reason? (I'm including Tay, of course.) Unlikely, perhaps; but not impossible. Look at that case in America. Anything's possible in the world to-day, Mrs. Fane. As I told you, it's not something I know a great deal about, but I do know a little. You'd be surprised."

Involuntarily, I jumped slightly. He said, "What's wrong?"

But it had gone. I shook my head. "I don't know. Something you said reminded me of something—something someone else said to me recently. But I can't remember what it was."

He did not drop it. "It was related to what we've been talking about?"

I tried again, but it evaded me. "I suppose it must have been. But it's no good. I can't remember."

Burgess tried several more questions, but without success. I just could not recall what had flashed through my mind. So he reverted to the subject of Giles. "You say he wouldn't give information to the Russians?"

"Oh, no," I said. "I don't think he would. Besides, he's never near the plant and he never comes to see any of us. So ho——"

I did not finish the question. Burgess understood easily. He said, "I know. *And* he wasn't at your uncle's dinner-party the night before the accident. He could, of course, be working with someone at the plant, but I don't see why, in that case——" He broke off. "Mrs. Fane, I'd like you to tell me something about the political ideas of your family."

"Political ideas? You mean which way they vote?"

"Yes. That. And the general nature of their beliefs—how seriously they take them. Begin—well, begin with yourself."

"Well, I'm—it's hard to explain. If I did, I'd have to go into very great detail. I was Labour at Cambridge and I voted for them in 1945. Since then, I've voted Liberal. I don't know what I'll do next time." Involuntarily, I smiled slightly and Burgess asked what was funny.

"Giles. He forgave me a lot because I voted Labour in 1945, but he was furious with me for voting Liberal. He said I should at least vote Conservative—and be loyal to the side that was feeding me. I told him Uncle Hugh didn't mind—that he was buying my brains and my time, not my soul. I also said that politics wasn't a religion with my uncle the way it was with him—that when Uncle Hugh felt religious, he went to church on Sundays. Giles was furious."

Burgess said he could imagine it. "But was it true?" he asked. "After all, the Freemen of Britain was in the nature of a crusade."

"I know. But I don't think my uncle was emotionally involved with them—not like that man, Gresham. I'd guess that Uncle Hugh simply decided that that was the best way to get the kind of government he thought necessary in Britain—and joined them. I should think there was very little emotion involved."

"It's possible, of course," said Burgess. "Well, go on. What about the rest?"

"My Uncle William is what is known as a crusted Tory—I don't think he ever thought about it much. He just takes it for granted that the right-wing of the Tory party is the place for anyone sensible—by which he means himself. My Aunt Mildred"—I laughed—"she's the kind of Tory who makes even good Tories think of voting Labour. Andrew—I suppose Andrew's a middle-of-the-road Tory. He's not very much interested in politics, but he's intelligent and not fanatical about the subject. Daphne votes Conservative because she knows all nice people do—she's never thought about it in her life. But to do her justice she isn't anything like Aunt Mildred."

"I see. And the others?"

"Robert's a Conservative M.P., as you know. I should say he was in the middle of the party, too—perhaps a shade to the left of Andrew. I don't know about Anne—I imagine she thinks much as Andrew does, but I don't remember talking politics with her recently. I think Charles is a Liberal, but you can't tell with him."

"He's a clever man, your cousin Charles. It's a moot point whether he's too clever."

I was silent. The news about the leakage at Uncle Hugh's plant had shocked me so much that I had emerged temporarily from my determination to keep as clear of the investigation as possible, and to tell Burgess the very minimum. Besides, my uncertainty touched only my personal life and my personal relations, not my political convictions. I had been genuinely appalled at Burgess' information and entirely clear that the source of the leakage must be discovered. But Burgess' remark about Charles had again brought the focus on murder and my new clarity of thought vanished. I got up to go.

"You know, Mrs. Fane," said Burgess, "you can be quite helpful when you try. It's a pity you don't try more often."

IX

Lunch was our least successful meal to date. The tension between Robert and Daphne had not lessened and they continued to ignore each other ostentatiously. Everyone but Charles and Tay seemed to take Giles' presence as a personal affront. A few barbs were directed at me by Aunt Mildred, who was under the mistaken impression that I had extended to Giles a pressing invitation to stay. Uncle William addressed one sentence to Giles: "Are you going to the funeral?" Giles with greater brevity said no. Uncle William grunted and that ended that exchange. Conversation in general was almost non-existent.

Nor could I bring myself to say anything. The conversation with Burgess had left me feeling wretched and I felt that any effort would be too much for me. One of us was a murderer and either that one or someone else was a traitor. I could hardly bear to remain at the table. I should have been feeling anger, outrage, and the conviction that the guilty person—or persons—must be caught and punished. I had felt that way about the person responsible for the information leakage when I had been talking to Burgess about it. But now all I could feel was lethargy—and extreme depression. I wanted to be away from everyone. I did not want to have to think about anything.

I found an occupation for the afternoon in sorting Uncle Hugh's papers. The police had already been through them, and had no objection to my doing some general arranging. It was a tedious, impersonal sort of job and I welcomed it. After I had been at it for over an hour, Tay found me there and offered to help. I needed some assistance, but I thought that if he talked about the murder, I would get up and walk out.

Tay did not. He settled down and methodically and intelligently helped me to sort and to file. Not until we had finished the tea that had been brought in to us did he talk about anything but our work. Then he said, almost idly, "Very Freudian situation, isn't it?"

"Why specifically Freudian?"

"The young men of the tribe kill the father or the chief. Sir Hugh was the chief and there are the young men—Charles, Andrew, Giles."

He made it sound like an impersonal situation, somewhat abstract, with no real people involved. I said, listlessly, "You're forgetting three other related suspects: Uncle William, Daphne, and myself—not to mention you."

He waved my remark aside as of no importance. "Of all of them, of course, Giles is the most likely. Certainly his relation with your uncle has the most Freudian overtones."

"Have you told your theories to Inspector Burgess?"

"No. But Burgess is no fool. I've no doubt he knows it."

"Do you think he also knows you gave those notes to Daphne?"

"I didn't," said Tay, emotionlessly.

"We disagree on that," I said. "Of course, I know Daphne can't prove her story—and it's your word against hers. She didn't happen to tell you what was on her mind, did she?"

"I have no idea what's on Daphne's mind," said Tay, precisely. "It is quite evident there is something. She would not have made a good actress."

I gave it up.

"In any event," Tay went on, "I'll be glad when Burgess finishes his investigation. The atmosphere in this house can hardly be improved by having Giles as an unwilling and largely unwelcome guest. And I'd like the matter of the business to be settled."

"I daresay you would," I agreed. "But it's all right for a few days, isn't it—the business, I mean? There's nothing crucial or urgent that has to be settled during the next few days, is there?"

Tay gave me an odd look. "No," he said. "Why should there be?"

I was too depressed to pursue it further. "No reason," I said. "I just asked."

The armed peace which had existed at lunch broke down entirely at dinner. I suppose the long strain of waiting had been exacerbated by Giles' presence; not that my cousin actually did anything. His things, together with some books and papers, were brought to him in the early afternoon, and he shut himself up in his room to work till tea-time. He then emerged, and after having a cup of tea, spent some time looking around the house. My Uncle William suggested to me caustically that Giles was no doubt doing a little amateur detecting. But I doubt that he was. Giles had been brought up at Feathers, after all, and in spite of any feelings he might have had about it now, he must have liked it once—or at least taken it for granted in the unquestioning way of children. He probably wanted to see it again at his leisure, and as he no doubt thought it unlikely he would again be at Feathers, he was using the opportunity to do just that.

However, his casual wanderings through the rooms on the ground floor seemed to have exasperated almost everyone. Perhaps it brought to the surface the resentment that Giles had, as my aunt persistently put it, "turned against his own class". Perhaps Giles' obvious familiarity with the house reminded various of his relations of what they would have preferred to forget: that no matter what he did, he was by birth and upbringing very closely connected with them.

So, by dinner, almost everyone was ready to have a go at Giles. Though I would have expected the first blow to come from my Aunt Mildred or my Uncle William, it in fact came from Tay. He said to Giles, with apparent amiability, "How does it feel to be back in your old home, Giles?"

"It's interesting," said Giles. "It's a survival from a past age. The days of this kind of house are really gone for ever—now that you can't get dozens of underpaid servants to staff it."

"Hugh always paid his servants very well," said Uncle William, turning red. His flushing was not specifically due to anger at Giles' remark—though, of course, he was angry. But for years, Uncle William had flushed with anger at the mere mention of Giles' name; so it was hardly likely he would not when flung such a challenging remark. "And servants in this country are free to leave when they like, anyway. Not like in Russia. Imagine a servant giving notice to Stalin!"

I looked around the table quickly at that. Though I did not glance at Burgess, I could guess he was alert and watchful. But no one seemed upset at the remark, and Uncle William snorted at his own wit.

The thing might have ended there, except for Tay, who took it up again. "There are a few things about your political beliefs that have never been quite clear to me, Giles. And since we meet so seldom, this seems a very good opportunity to clarify them. You object to a house like Feathers because it costs a lot of money to buy and to run—even with underpaid servants. Yet you surely don't advocate equality of income in your magazine. At least, from all I've heard, you make a very good income—and so do some of your friends. I don't know what you do with your money, and, of course, it's none of my business. But if someone, instead of spending an income as large as yours, saves enough of it to buy a house like Feathers and then runs it on the income instead of—well, whatever else you can do, drinking expensive liquor and gambling—why is that wrong?"

"I'm afraid you haven't been reading Giles' writings carefully," said Andrew, before Giles could speak. "An income of £5,000 a year is wrong if it's earned—or made, let's say—by Uncle Hugh or by you or by me. But if it's made by someone who has the welfare of the people at heart and says so, that's all right. Furthermore, to spend a lot of money if you make it is all right. But to save it is wrong—because that way you accumulate it and leave it to your children—and they become privileged."

"Well, you've part of it right anyway," said Giles, "which I suppose is a miracle." He was very angry, but he kept his voice under control. "I'm not in favour of equality of incomes. But I'm in favour of children starting out equally; and if their parents accumulate a lot of property and pass it on to them, then children don't start out equally. That's why I favour raising inheritance taxes—so that it's almost impossible to leave any property to one's children."

"Perhaps you really favour huge inheritance taxes," said my aunt, bitingly, "because you know Hugh hasn't left you anything!"

Now as long as the discussion had been largely political, Giles had kept his head. Tay had done him somewhat less than justice, and considering that he was the object of a three-pronged attack, Giles had controlled himself fairly well. But on the subject of Uncle Hugh, he was never moderate; and he was not now. He turned on my aunt a look so withering that almost anyone else might have winced. But since my aunt's dislike for him was at least as strong as his for her, she remained unmoved.

"You and your little mind!" he said. "You would think that! All you think about is money. All you ever talked about to your children was money—and all that you thought went with it. You pretend to be sorry Uncle Hugh's dead—when all the time you're secretly gloating in your minds over all the money you'll have now. Hugh kept a pretty tight rein on the capital, didn't he? Must have bothered you all. I wouldn't put it past any of you to have murdered him just on that account. Hugh didn't leave me any money—I'd have been insulted if he had! I wouldn't touch any of his dirty money and neither would any other decent person!"

If Burgess had thought anyone would be stunned by this outburst, he had underestimated my family—and Tay. There was a general tightness around the table, but that was all. And Tay said, "Well, you've conducted investigations into the way your uncle got his money for some time now, and even you have never made out a case that proves he got it dishonestly. As to his having been murdered for his money—at least, no one's been heard threatening to murder him on that account—and you openly threatened to murder him for his political activities!"

This time there was a brief, appalled silence. For no one knew of this threat, so far as I was aware, but Burgess, Tay, myself and—of course—Giles. But before Giles could answer, Andrew cut in. "It's generally known that people who make open threats don't carry them out," he said, "though in the future, Giles, I'd be careful if I were you to see that there are no—outside eavesdroppers about. I suppose," he said to Burgess, "people who make open threats are much less dangerous than those who work—underground?"

Burgess said rather primly that he did not know. He could hardly have escaped the implication in Andrew's uncharacteristic defence of Giles: the outsider who worked underground was easily identifiable as Tay. And if Tay's rather blatant attempt to show Giles to Burgess at my cousin's intemperate worst was evident, so was Andrew's determination to express his own opinion of Tay.

Giles was not noticeably grateful for Andrew's sudden intervention on his behalf. "When thieves fall out!" he said. "Well, it's a pretty picture."

He would probably have gone on at some length and in some detail. But Charles interrupted him smoothly. "I imagine the Inspector finds all this a pretty picture," he remarked, gently. "But life in the effete diplomatic circles in which I move has unfitted me for this rugged verbal warfare. Perhaps we could all adjourn for coffee and a less barbed conversation."

I rose. "It's a very good idea," I said. "We'll have coffee in the drawing-room. That should calm things a bit. I know you'd be willing to shoot some of us in front of the firing squad, Giles, but I'm sure your early training went too deep for you to be able to brawl in front of the servants."

Giles gave me an angry and a suspicious look. Then he grinned reluctantly, and we all went into the drawing-room for coffee. I wondered what Burgess had made of that episode.

As I learned later, Burgess was at that stage very much confused. He had, if anything, too much information, and it had not yet fallen into a recognizable pattern. He was an astute and patient man, and very determined. It never occurred to him that he would not solve the case eventually; but at that stage his ideas had not yet assumed any pattern. He was appalled at the intrusion of the espionage element into the affair. It had shaken even the very tentative ideas he had begun to form. He did not know whether he had one case or two.

Much later, when we discussed the matter, Burgess told us something of his impressions of all of us. They were different from mine and different from what I had expected. I had believed that from the beginning he considered some of us more likely to murder than others. But I had known Tay and my family all my life. So the differences between us were much clearer to me than the similarities. Burgess was more impressed by the similarities.

Burgess saw us all—and particularly the younger generation—as self-centred, self-willed, and over-indulged. He thought that we all had had our own way for so long that we might easily react violently to being seriously thwarted. He thought, too, that we were so spoiled that almost any deviation—political or otherwise—might be possible. He did not share my assumption that most of us were incapable of murder. More, he thought the advantages all of us would gain from Uncle Hugh's death financially alone were sufficient to drive even far less egocentric people to murder. Nor did our behaviour to each other change these rather unflattering judgments, though I think that as he came to know us better, he could perceive the differences between us more clearly. They never, however, seemed as evident to him as they did to us.

Further, Burgess was not uninformed about politics. He knew how difficult it was to detect a dedicated Communist—if there was one among us—behind our masks. Straightforward murder he could deal with; he was accustomed to it. But the combination of murder and espionage in a group like ours was very tricky. He did not underestimate the difficulties.

Burgess was still further handicapped by the very thoroughness of his investigation and the investigations made for him in London. He was not satisfied with knowing only what we would tell him about ourselves or about each other, plus what his men could pick up in the village or from the servants. So detectives in London made some swift enquiries into our lives, and sent the details on to him. (They had barely started to look for clues that might reveal the source of the information leakage.) Meanwhile, Burgess spent most of Tuesday afternoon and evening digesting such information as he already had, and trying to fit it in with his experiences since Sunday and with his impressions of all of us. He had to reduce it in some way to a pattern that made sense. By late Tuesday night the task still looked formidable.

Wednesday morning, I went for a walk in the grounds before breakfast. It was a pleasant, sunny day. As I was coming back and about to re-enter the house, I saw a figure coming towards me. I thought it was a reporter and waited to intercept him.

It was a young man. He said good morning politely. "It's lucky I found you," he said. "I was afraid no one was up yet. I've come to see Mr. Randall."

"I'm sorry," I said. "I'm afraid you can't. We aren't having any visitors at the house for the present."

"Well, I'm not exactly a visitor. I'm a friend of Giles. You must be his cousin."

"One of them."

"I thought I'd seen you with him. You're Mrs. Fane, aren't you?"

"Yes. And I'm afraid I'll have to ask you to leave. As I told you, we're not having any visitors just now."

"But I have to see Giles. It's about his Defence Committee."

"His *what*?"

"His Defence Committee. Bella Moore called me, you see. She explained everything. I've just come to arrange details with Giles—to make sure he gets the best possible defence."

"Defence against what?"

My visitor considered me wilfully obtuse. "He'll need to be properly defended on this murder charge, of course."

"You were told he had been charged with murder?"

"No. Bella said he hadn't been charged yet, but that it was obviously heading that way. Naturally, with his views, he could hardly expect a fair deal, could he? We wanted to get started right away. We'll see he gets a fair trial—but we'll have to raise money to do it. Giles makes a lot, of course, but I don't suppose he saves it. And justice comes expensive in this country."

"You mean to say you think he'll get justice," I asked, ironically, "with the class-system at work in the selection of judges?"

"We understand that difficulty," he assured me, seriously. "But we'll get enough publicity to make the judge think twice before he renders an obviously prejudiced judgment."

I stared at him. He was completely sure of himself. He *knew* that virtue resided alone in his friends and himself. No reasonable, honest answer would have convinced him. My normal reaction—the one that had been normal to me for the last few years—would have been merely to tell him again that no visitors were being received at the house. But as I looked at his positive, patronizing face, I was suddenly shaken by a blazing rage.

"Now you listen to me," I said. "Giles is not under arrest. He is under suspicion as much or as little as the rest of us. If the police do arrest him for murder, it will be because they believe they have convincing evidence, not because he has certain political views. This is still England, you know—or have you come to believe your own propaganda? And if Giles should be arrested, his family will see that he has the best possible legal advice. Do you think we'd allow him to be used for the purposes of political propaganda by you and your friends—when his life might be in danger? Now get out of here!"

My anger had startled him as much as it startled me. He went.

When he had gone, I did not go back to the house immediately. I was still angry; but it was the lesser part of what I was feeling. I felt as if some block or inhibition in me had, with that outburst, broken completely. For the first time in years, I had responded quickly and with assurance to a new situation in which I was myself involved. It was as if, after a winding and tortuous journey, I had found myself again. I was wildly exhilarated and I felt as if I had been drinking. My mind touched the ghost of Simon lightly and I did not wince. It was all right, at last.

I must have stayed there for some time. I was not conscious of minutes passing. Eventually, I realized that I was very hungry and I went back to the house.

My entire family was in the dining-room. Everyone was wearing black except Giles, who had even refused all offers of black ties. I helped myself to a large breakfast and sat down. Everyone was very subdued and quiet, and I felt that my recent almost jubilant happiness was very much out of place. But I was still aware of it.

I had started to drink my second cup of coffee when Mrs. Rapp came in. She looked truculent. My Aunt Mildred, taking no notice of this, immediately began to issue various and confusing orders for the day. This had happened so often before that everyone took it for granted. But I did not. I interrupted before my aunt had spoken three sentences.

"I've already spoken to Mrs. Rapp, Aunt Mildred," I said. "And I think she understands quite well what to do. It's very difficult for her if she has to try to follow several sets of instructions from different people. Suppose we let things go on as they are until after lunch. Then we'll all know—where we stand."

There were one or two gasps. Everyone looked at me as if I had just announced my conversion to some exotic creed. For a moment, I thought my aunt was ready to give battle. In my mood, I think I would have welcomed it. But she decided against it and left the table without another word, followed by her husband. No one else said anything about the matter. When I left the room after finishing my breakfast, Charles, who was lingering over his coffee, sprang to his feet to open the door. He gave me a decorous wink as I passed him.

I went straight to the sitting-room to find Burgess. "Have you a few moments to talk to me?" I asked. "This may not be the best time for it, but there are a few things I feel I ought to tell you—though I've no idea whether they'll be any use to you or not."

Burgess looked at me sharply. "Has something happened?" he asked.

"Nothing to do with my uncle's murder—nor with anything at the plant. It's only—it's just occurred to me that I've been behaving rather unintelligently. You must solve this case—and the sooner the better for all of us. If I can help you, I will."

What I could tell him did not add up to much. I told him about my interviews with Giles and Bella, with Andrew and Anne. I recounted my conversation with Tay in the library, and added that though I had no proof, I believed Tay had given Daphne the money in return for a promise to vote any shares his way. I described my meeting with Giles' defender earlier in the morning; and for the sake of thoroughness, added my conflict with my aunt over Mrs. Rapp.

Burgess laughed over the last, but he asked me a number of pertinent questions about the other things I had told him. He said, then, "Your cousin, Mrs. Alison, has been behaving very strangely. Do you know why?"

"I've not any evidence," I said, slowly. "But I have an idea. I've known Daphne all my life, and I can only think of one sort of trouble she'd be likely to get herself into."

"Something to do with a man, you mean?"

"Yes."

"It's an accurate guess, Mrs. Fane. She has. At least, she's got herself involved with a man, though I don't yet know the exact nature of her difficulty."

"An author of some sort?"

"How did you know?"

"I didn't. But a friend of mine said something to me one day—weeks ago—about seeing her at an Authors' League luncheon. That sort of thing isn't at all Daphne's line. So I assumed she must be interested in a man whose line it was."

"You'd have saved me a certain amount of trouble if you'd told me that before, Mrs. Fane. Yes. It's an author. His name's Philip Denton—writes novels. Do you know him?"

"I've met him." I was surprised. "He's very nice. I can't imagine what she—anyway, he's been out of the country for some months, hasn't he? I remember reading it in the papers."

"That's right. He went to America about two months ago or so."

I shook my head. "It doesn't make any sense to me. I'll try to talk to Daphne to-day, if you like—though there won't be much time till after the will's been read."

"It might help. I shall find out, of course. But I'd prefer not to bully it out of her, if I can help it. By the way, Mrs. Fane"—he looked at something in his folder—"do you happen to know a scientist at your uncle's factory called Edward Bryce?"

"Edward Bryce," I repeated. "I don't—oh, yes. I've met him. He's a friend of Charles—I think Charles got him his job, as a matter of fact. Why? Is it important?"

"I don't know yet," said Burgess. "Now there's one final thing, Mrs. Fane. You remember that on Sunday night I told you I thought one or two of the servants might be holding something back. I asked you to talk to Mrs. Rapp about it and you more or less said you wouldn't. Will you, now?"

"You mean—right away?"

"Yes—and in front of me."

I said all right, and a policeman was sent to find Mrs. Rapp. She came in, looking impressive in black. I said, "Mrs. Rapp, Mr. Burgess seems to have the idea that you didn't tell him quite everything you knew the other day. I don't know whether that's so or not. But if it is—if you're trying to protect someone, anyone—it'd be far better if you didn't. We must find out the truth, you know. I've told the Inspector everything I know, and I very much wish you'd do the same."

I don't know how much effect I would have had, had I said this to her before my conflict with my aunt at breakfast. But the housekeeper looked at me for a moment and then said, "No matter who is involved, Mrs. Fane? Did you mean that?"

"Yes," I said. "You know, whatever it is—it may not mean what you think it does at all."

Mrs. Rapp considered that, and nodded. "All right," she said. "Well, I can tell it to you—you won't have to call in anyone else. It was Saturday night—or early Sunday morning, I should say. I wasn't sleeping very well, and I heard someone come in—just about five o'clock or maybe a few minutes later. Then, when one of the maids was doing the shoes in the morning, she said to me—in the kitchen—'Funny Mr. Charles' shoes being muddy—hasn't been raining.' I said, 'It's because you're young you sleep like that. It rained about an hour this morning. Mr. Charles must have had trouble sleeping and gone out for a walk.' I didn't think anything of it at the time, of course. But when all this happened, I did think of it—and I told the girl not to say anything." She looked not at Burgess but at me. "I hope it's all right, Miss Christy. I wouldn't want to get Mr. Charles into any trouble."

I thought that this would have come out sooner or later; and that, in a way, it could count as much in Charles' favour as against it. I said, "I don't think you've got Mr. Charles into any special trouble. And thank you for telling us."

She left. Burgess regarded me thoughtfully. "Interesting," he said. But he added nothing more.

X

The funeral went off without incident. There were scores of reporters near the church, but we evaded them without too much difficulty and came back to the house. I would have expected lunch to be the worst of the many strained and uneasy meals we had had together. To my surprise, it turned out to be one of the smoothest—probably because the funeral was over and the reading of the will soon would be. The question of the murder, which had had first place in all our minds since early Sunday morning, had now temporarily been shelved. Uncle Hugh's solicitor, Edward Temple, had come down for the funeral, and he had lunch with us. It was all very polite and decorous, and even Giles managed to say one or two civil words.

We had selected the dining-room—where we could all sit around the table and take notes if we wished—as the most convenient place for the will to be read. The solicitor sat at the head, his papers and documents in front of him. On one side, Charles sat next to him. Then came myself, Giles, Daphne, and Robert. Uncle William was on Temple's other side, followed by Aunt Mildred, Andrew, Anne, and Tay. Inspector Burgess sat at the foot of the table. The room was quiet; and Temple, after explaining that it was a valid will, duly witnessed, giving its date and other preliminary information, read out the long and complicated document.

My Uncle Hugh's sense of humour, his generosity, and his unusual character, were all evident in the provisions of the will. There were generous amounts given to charity, to the staff at Feathers, and to other people who had served him or worked with him. There then followed the disposal of his personal fortune (after provision for death duties). The first surprise came here. Uncle Hugh left 40 per cent of his personal fortune to Charles, 20 per cent to me, 10 per cent each to Uncle William, Daphne, and Andrew—and 10 per cent to be held in trust until their twenty-fifth birthdays to any children Giles might have. The library was divided between Charles and me, the London house and all my uncle's personal belongings went to his son—and Feathers went to me.

But more was to come. The tension around the table was mounting as Temple, in his precise, unemotional voice, read out my uncle's disposal of the non-voting shares in the company. Half went to Charles, 25 per cent to me, and the rest went equally to the children of Daphne, Andrew, and—again—any children Giles might have. I was aware of Giles' outraged but suppressed protest, and of Burgess' careful eyes seeing all of us and our reactions.

We came at last to the voting shares of the company. Here was my uncle's final and most enjoyable projection. He must have savoured it fully. He divided the shares into four equal parts: one to Charles, one to me, one to Andrew, and one to Daphne's children, to be held in trust for twenty years and to be voted by Tay. Any voting shares in the company held by outsiders were negligible and widely scattered. With Andrew and Tay at loggerheads—as they were—it meant in essence that final control rested with Charles' votes—or with mine; or that, should Charles and I wish to act together, we could probably put in anyone we chose to run the company.

I looked at the faces around the table. Both Tay and Andrew were clearly appalled. Both of them had been hoping that at least the thing would finally be settled, one way or the other. To have the situation continued—to see the possibility of its continuing for years, even decades—must have seemed intolerable. Giles, though for different reasons, looked almost equally appalled, and I could well imagine what some of the press unfriendly to him would make of it: "Left-winger's

Unborn Children Inherit Fortune". My uncle had undoubtedly relished just that sort of headline—in anticipation—though that was probably not the only reason he had left money to Giles' children. He had, after all, not discontinued Giles' allowance; it had been Giles who had refused to accept any money.

Uncle William and Aunt Mildred looked outraged, both at the possibility of future conflict in the company and at what they considered to be the slights to their children—and the ill-judged favouring of Charles and me. Both of them had said so often that Andrew was obviously the son Uncle Hugh had wanted that they were shocked at his leaving more property to his son than to anyone else. For some inexplicable reason, too, my aunt had been convinced that Uncle Hugh would leave Feathers either to Uncle William or to Andrew. The thought that it had been left to me—which surprised me as much as it did her—was difficult for her to bear without comment.

Charles, the greatest beneficiary of all this, sat there with an absolutely expressionless face. But at his first moment of realization—when he first became aware that his father had left him a quarter-share in the company plus all the other property—he had flushed to the roots of his hair. I had not seen Charles blush since he was a boy of sixteen, and I could not even guess what had moved him so much.

Temple finished his reading, removed his glasses, and sat back with a self-satisfied smile. My Uncle William was the first to speak. "But— that will's an outrage!" he spluttered. "It's fantastic!"

Temple, who had been polishing his glasses, put them on again and looked at my uncle. "I thought it an entirely correct and intelligent will," he said, coldly. "Very generous, too."

Uncle William started to speak again, but Andrew stopped him. "My father is a bit surprised at some of the provisions," he said. "I think we all are. It makes some complications as regards—control of the company. Still, we'll probably work it out satisfactorily—especially since there is no doubt at all that the will is entirely valid and makes exactly the provisions Uncle Hugh intended. I agree with you, sir, that it is very generous."

"Intelligent and generous!" said Giles. "You'll have civil war at that company for twenty years and that's your idea of wisdom and generosity! What did Hugh do to you—hypnotize you? And leaving money to any children I might have! Well, at least I can stop that. I can refuse to have them accept it."

"I'm afraid you're entirely mistaken, Mr. Randall," said Temple, his voice even colder than before. "That money is for your children, when they reach the designated age. Should they wish to refuse it then, that is entirely their own affair, and you can, of course, influence them in any way you like. But you can't refuse it for them."

"And somehow I don't think they will," said Andrew, with some malice.

My aunt was still very much offended. She would no doubt continue to be for some time. She said, addressing no one in particular, "Well, since the police still haven't said we could leave, I presume we are trespassing on Christy's hospitality—that is, if she will continue to have us."

Her voice was almost venomous. Anne looked at me with some amusement. I said, "Naturally, you will all remain until the police have finished their investigation."

"And, of course, you will now see that the servants are properly instructed."

"Yes."

Charles apparently decided that the exhibition of family manners had gone far enough. He thanked Mr. Temple for his trouble and added that he hoped the solicitor would continue to handle his own legal affairs and those of any other member of the family who wished him to do so. My cousin said he presumed that Mr. Temple would let anyone know of any documents which needed signatures or any other technical arrangements which it would be necessary to make regarding the transfer of property. Temple was mollified by this civil approach. He said a few polite words in reply, and the meeting was over. Everyone went off, Burgess included, and I was left with Temple. I asked if he would like to stay to tea.

"It's very kind of you, Mrs. Fane," he said. "But I really must get back to London."

"Raikes will take you to the station."

"Thank you, Mrs. Fane. You know, you needn't feel any concern over inheriting this house. Your uncle always intended to leave it to you. He thought you liked it."

"He was right. I do. It's unexpected, though. I shall probably take some time getting used to the idea that it belongs to me."

Temple did not reply. When he next spoke, he seemed embarrassed. "That will was some years old, as you know," he said. "I don't know whether your uncle planned to change it or not. The police came to see me in London. They spoke of a large gift he might have been planning to make to—an organization. He never spoke to me of it. But it is true that he did ask a number of questions about the form such gifts might take—and there is no doubt that there would have been far-reaching effects, had he carried out his idea."

"Yes," I said. "Do you think it would have damaged the business badly?"

"I'm not really qualified to judge. My own opinion would be that it would, however. You see, he was talking in terms of a big gift. That would have meant turning over a lot of capital and couldn't have been good for the business. Besides, there's something else. The English react oddly, you know. I don't think this idea of Sir Hugh's would have gone down well either with the business community or with the man in the street. The effect of a good deal of ill-will on the business might have been considerable."

"Naturally," I said.

This merely confirmed what Gresham had said. If Uncle Hugh had lived to make the Freemen the large gift he had contemplated, if he had become publicly active in the organization as he had planned, his financial position and that of the company might both have been badly shaken. Had this happened, all of us would have been much worse off than we were going to be as matters stood. Presumably none of us had checked these facts with Temple. But most of us were capable of working them out for ourselves, in general if not in detail. There was no doubt that from the point of view of his legatees, Uncle Hugh had picked a very suitable moment to die. If motive alone constituted grounds for an accusation of murder, no doubt all of us could stand in the dock together.

At that point, I thought the party at Feathers resembled nothing so much as an Italian opera taking place on a large stage. Small groups congregated in various spots, discussing the will and its probable effects. Andrew and Uncle William stood together in one corner of the library, no doubt discussing the next step as regards the business. Aunt Mildred had taken Daphne off to her bedroom, to expatiate on the iniquities of her late brother-in-law. Charles and Anne, in another corner of the library, stood looking out of the window and having a civil talk in which neither appeared to be much interested. Tay and Robert were exchanging neutral remarks, and Giles was sitting in a large chair, saying nothing at all.

When I came in, Charles turned to me with a grin. "The one thing we really need is a drink, Christy. It's your house—do you approve of the idea?"

"Yes," I said. I was going to ring for the butler, but Charles stopped me and said he would fetch them himself. Anne said to me, "Well, what are you going to do—now that you've got money and this huge house? Travel? Go in for good works? Settle down at Feathers and become the *grande dame* of the neighbourhood?"

"I don't know," I said. "I haven't got that far yet. Have you any suggestions?"

"My family," said Anne, "distrusts women on their own—especially women with a lot of money. If this were my family, they'd be gathered together working out a way to get you married off soon—to keep you out of trouble."

I smiled. "Would anyone in your family leave a will like that?"

"I don't suppose so. By the next generation, though, none of you will. You'll be very much like us then."

"And what would your family do," I asked, "about the situation as it now stands?"

She did not pretend to misunderstand. "They'd take it for granted that a family sticks together. That's the only way to get on top and stay there. The solution's quite simple, after all."

"You mean Charles and I should both throw our support to Andrew and get rid of Tay? And then let Andrew take over?"

"Of course. Charles doesn't want to run the company—at least, he's never given any signs of it. Neither, I take it, do you. Tay has plenty of money, so there's no problem there. He engaged in a gamble and it didn't come off. Well, he'll live through it."

In a way, she was perfectly right. But whether Charles and I threw our support either to Andrew or to Tay, the situation would not be satisfactory. Men as ambitious as those two would hardly be satisfied with a control that depended on the good will of either Charles or me, even assuming we both acted together. In the beginning, in gratitude, they might resolve to be entirely fair and just to us. Gradually, however, they would try to work out some way of gaining permanent control that was not dependent on either of us. Nor could I blame them if they did. When one's life is wrapped up in something, it is difficult to feel that it could be taken away at any moment by an outsider. I could hardly ask Anne whether she thought Tay or Andrew more likely to run the company more efficiently or more likely to be fair to his supporters. Andrew was my cousin, even though we were not particularly close. Tay had more experience in running the business. It was not as simple a decision for me as Anne seemed to think it should be.

"Just for the sake of discussion," I said, "suppose it didn't work that way. What would you advise Andrew to do?"

"To get out," said Anne, promptly. "I don't see that there's a difficult decision to make at all. Either you and Charles support him—as, of course, I think you should—and he stays. Or else you refuse or are dubious—in which case he gets out. Andrew has his own money now and he's very able. He can build up a business of his own. It may not reach the proportions of your Uncle Hugh's, but at least it would be his own."

Or, translated: make up your mind, Christy. If Andrew can't have control, he can always leave. Tay is getting on, and he isn't well. If you back Tay and Andrew leaves, Tay may have to leave as well in a couple of years. He's hardly likely to be active in the business more than ten years, and then you and Charles can look for someone else. Whether you can find someone as capable and as devoted to all our interests as Andrew is another matter. But whatever you do, I shan't turn a hair, and I shall advise Andrew not to either.

I had no time to answer, for Charles came back with the drinks, and a general reshuffle took place. Aunt Mildred and Daphne reappeared, and Daphne and Anne went into the garden with their glasses in hand. Aunt Mildred, who did not believe in drinking "under the circumstances", appropriated the desk to write some letters. Robert, Charles, and Uncle William went off to play billiards. Giles, who would have preferred to remain in the library, but would not stay in the same room with Aunt Mildred willingly, took a book and went off. I went into the kitchen to see Mrs. Rapp.

For some reason, Mrs. Rapp and the cook had decided that an elaborate dinner was in order. Whether the housekeeper was celebrating her release from nagging by my aunt or whether she just felt a good dinner would have a fortunate psychological effect, I don't know. In any event, she presented to me a long and complicated menu and suggested that I might care to choose the wines, having a look at the wine-cellar as I did so.

I realized with surprise that my uncle's very impressive wine-cellar at Feathers was now my property. I doubt whether any member of our family, before Uncle Hugh, had ever drunk any wine outside of an occasional and very bad tawny port. But Uncle Hugh himself had liked all aspects of good living, including wine, and had contrived to learn a good deal about the subject during his life. His cellar was extensive and well chosen.

My own taste in wine was similar to that of my late uncle. So, together with the butler, I spent an absorbed hour, selecting the wines for dinner, looking over the stock, and listening to his grave suggestions for future purchases. Sanderson appeared to take it for granted that the establishment at Feathers would go on precisely as it had during my uncle's lifetime, and as I had not yet made up my mind on this point, I did not contradict him. We worked our way gradually to the back and darkest section of the cellar, and were about to conclude our tour when Sanderson caught sight of a small, yellowish paper tucked in between the bottles. He reached out, took it, opened it, and read it. Then he frowned in perplexity, read it again, and handed it to me without a word.

The paper was a telegram. It was dated Saturday and addressed to my cousin Andrew. The message was completely incomprehensible. It had been sent from London, and read: "George tricky stop suggest Peter Able." It was unsigned.

It was not difficult to work out what had happened. That telegram had apparently arrived for Andrew and he had not wanted it to be found. Presumably he also had not wanted it to be destroyed. The house was filled with policemen, and there was no guessing when they might decide to make a search. They had made several already. So Andrew had apparently decided to hide the telegram in what he had every reason to think a safe place, and to retrieve it later. Normally, it would have been a good choice, for no one went into the wine-cellar but the butler and Uncle Hugh. The recess in which the telegram had been hidden might well go unvisited for weeks. It was Andrew's bad luck that it had not. What the telegram meant and why he had secreted it, I did not even bother to consider. That was Burgess' job; and I did not hesitate. I took the telegram to him directly and explained to him the circumstances under which it had been found.

Burgess read the telegram several times. It obviously made no more sense to him than it had to me. "You've no idea what it means, Mrs. Fane?"

"No."

"George tricky stop suggest Peter Able." He considered it. "Sounds a bit like code, doesn't it? Do you know anyone called Peter Able?"

"No."

"I wonder if your cousin Andrew does?"

I did not answer. Burgess put the telegram in his pocket. "I wonder if you'd mind showing me where you found it. And by the way, Mrs. Fane, can I rely on you not to say anything to anyone about it?"

"Yes," I said. "You can. Perhaps you'd better have a word with Sanderson, though."

When I had shown Burgess where I had found the telegram, and left him in the wine-cellar, I came back upstairs. I noticed that the afternoon post had been placed on the hall table. There was a large pile of letters, many of them notes of condolence to various members of the family. My cousin Daphne had picked up some of the letters and was going through them with violent haste. I said, "What d'you think you're doing?"

She jumped at the sound of my voice. "Oh, it's you, Christy. I'm— expecting a letter—it must be here somewhere. I thought I'd—well, I'm rather in a hurry to get it."

"So much in a hurry," I said, "that you seem to have taken leave of your common sense. You know that Burgess expects to see the post before anyone else. He'd think it very odd if he could see you now. As a matter of fact, he thinks your entire behaviour odd, and I agree with him. I've been wanting to talk to you."

Daphne was still going through the letters frantically. "He hasn't any right——"

"Do stop talking like your mother," I said. "This is an investigation for murder and he has every right. In fact, he's been extraordinarily decent to you so far, but it can't go on much longer. As to your letter, if it's an innocent, ordinary one, there's no point in making such a fuss. And if—as I suppose—it isn't, there's certainly no sense in your going out of your way to call attention to it."

"No sense at all," said Burgess. He was standing behind us and he put out his hand for the letter Daphne was holding. In a daze, she handed it to him. Burgess did not give her time to have hysterics. He began to speak instantly, and his voice was sharp and incisive.

"Mrs. Alison," he said, "I dislike bullying anyone and I've been hoping that you would manage to use a little common sense. So far, you haven't—and I haven't the time to wait much longer. I know all about you and Philip Denton, so that needn't worry you. Now will you come along and answer my questions like a reasonable person or shall I get your husband and your parents along and see if they can help make some sense of things?"

His cool matter-of-factness, coupled with the threat in his last sentence, had an effect. Daphne looked from him to me. Then her shoulders sagged in a defeated way and she said, "Well, if you know that much—all right. Do you mind if Christy comes, too?"

"She seems to be present at a large number of interviews," said Burgess, dryly. "No, I don't mind."

In the small sitting-room, Burgess opened Daphne's letter. When he had read it, he handed it to her. She read it listlessly and gave it back to him. Burgess handed it to me. The letter was on ordinary writing-paper and was very brief. The writer acknowledged Daphne's letter posted Saturday and said he would expect the sum she mentioned within ten days. That was all. It was not signed.

"Well," said Burgess, "it's a simple enough explanation. I might have guessed. How much have you given this chap already? And how much more does he want?"

"I've given him £100," said my cousin, dully. "He wants another £1,000."

Burgess said something under his breath. "Why didn't you go to the police?"

"He said—if I did, he'd tell my husband."

Burgess sighed. "Mrs. Alison, that's what a police force is for. We have ways of dealing with blackmailers—we've had a lot of experience with them. What has he got of yours—letters, something?"

"Letters," said Daphne, in a low voice. "And he saw us once in a hotel—we'd registered—as if we were married."

Burgess sighed again. "What's his name, Mrs. Alison?"

My cousin, who had been quiet and apathetic up to this point, was startled into panic. "I can't tell you! I won't tell you! You'll go after him and he'll tell Robert. You didn't—I won't——" She burst into tears, and I got up and went over to her.

Burgess waited until she was calmer. "Mrs. Alison," he said, "I have to remind you again that this is an investigation for murder. You are being unnecessarily obstructive and I'm not in the mood for much more of it. However—I'll let the man's name go for now. I've a good deal else to discuss with you. But I plan to do it now," he added, his voice taking on a sharp note which made Daphne raise her head and look at him.

She made an effort. "I'm sorry. As long as I don't have to tell you his name——What else do you want to know?"

"The story. You had an affair with a man called Philip Denton. Then about two or three months ago, he went off to America. You can take it up at that point."

"Yes," said Daphne. "Well, he wanted me to go to America with him. But I—I didn't. I couldn't. Then, after he'd been gone for about a week, this man began to blackmail me. I was only able to give him small sums—ten pounds, twenty pounds. He kept threatening to tell Robert if I didn't get more. I had another letter from him on Friday, just before we came to Feathers, and I didn't have time to answer it. It made me—desperate. So I wrote him on Saturday morning, just before we went to play golf. I mailed it in the village, when we stopped for cigarettes."

"What did you say in the letter?"

"I didn't know what to say. I was—I didn't know what to do. So I just said I was staying at Feathers and if he'd give me ten days, I'd give him the money he'd asked for. That's all."

"Did you tell him you planned to get it from your uncle?"

"No."

"But you assumed he'd think so, since you were staying at Feathers?"

"I—suppose so."

"I see," said Burgess. "Now, when you went to see your uncle that night, did you plan to tell him? Or did you plan to get the money out of him without telling him?"

Daphne was a poor liar. She started several sentences, but they must have sounded unconvincing even to her, because she gave them up after a few words and sat silent. Burgess said he was still waiting and my cousin tried again.

"I went to his room—Gresham was right about that. I didn't think of telling him about the—the whole thing. I was afraid to—I couldn't tell him a thing like that. I didn't know what he'd do. I just said I needed some money and he wanted to know why. And I said I couldn't tell him."

"What was he like when you saw him? Did he seem in any way unusual—disturbed, unhappy, anything out of the ordinary?"

"No. He was much nicer than I'd thought he'd be. He said I'd obviously got into some trouble and I'd better tell him about it. He'd see what he could do to help me. I said I couldn't, and he said I should just go back to my room and think it over and we'd talk about it to-morrow—Sunday, that is."

"Then you were telling the truth? He didn't give you the money, Mr. Tay did?"

"Yes."

"In return for your promise to vote any shares you might get his way?"

Daphne reddened. "Yes." She did not ask him how he had known.

"If you hadn't dropped that money, you were planning to send it to your blackmailer?"

"Yes."

Burgess' voice was as pleasant and easy as if he had been discussing the weather. "What did you mean by the letter you wrote? I mean, how did you plan to get the money you promised him? Were you so sure your uncle would give it to you?"

"I wasn't sure. I thought—he might. But I just wrote it to keep him quiet for a while, so I could think of some other way to get it."

Daphne did not seem to realize the implications her words might have. I forced myself to listen to what Burgess was saying. He was talking about Philip Denton. "You saw a good deal of him. Where did you go together? What did you do?"

My cousin looked puzzled. "Oh, the usual sort of things. We went to the theatre and to films and out to dinner and to the country, and to Authors' League lunches." Her face looked quite different: younger and much happier. It had clearly been a happy time. Then she remembered where she was and what we were discussing, and her momentary joy vanished.

"I see," said Burgess. "Nothing out of the ordinary, then. Do you know what kind of friends he had, Mrs. Alison?"

She looked even more puzzled. "Just ordinary people. I mean— what do you want to know? They were like anyone else. Well, perhaps not quite—they weren't as stuffy as most of the people we know."

"How d'you mean, stuffy? Politically stuffy?"

"Politically——No. I mean, I don't know. They didn't talk politics. That's why I liked it so much—just jokes and general talk and nothing about what the government was going to do next. It was such a change." She sounded passionately grateful for the change. I thought that if all this were an act, if Daphne really were a Communist, she was even better at acting than Charles.

"And your friend Denton didn't talk politics either?"

Daphne appeared to consider. "I *think* Philip said he voted Conservative in the last election. But I'm not sure. We never talked politics."

Burgess decided to give it up. "All right, Mrs. Alison. Let's get back to this business of blackmail. You said you wrote this letter last Friday to quiet the man, so you could think of another way to get it. What way did you have in mind? Were you counting on the money you knew you'd inherit when your uncle died?"

Daphne again looked perplexed. "But I couldn't know how much I'd inherit. And anyway, everyone expected Uncle Hugh to live for years."

"Everyone," said Burgess, "but the person who killed him."

Daphne was very pale. "You sound as though you thought *I* killed him."

"No," said Burgess, judicially. "I'm not saying that. I'm saying that you had the opportunity and access to the means, like everyone else. And a very powerful motive."

"But you *can't* think I—I—would kill anyone. You must be out of your mind. Why, I——" She again seemed on the verge of tears. I said, "Don't get so excited, Daphne. The Inspector's not arresting you. He's just asking questions."

She seemed to regain control of herself quite quickly. She said, in her normal voice, "Anyway, you can't think I murdered him. It's impossible. And besides, you must know who did it by now. I thought you did know and were just looking for proof."

It was Burgess' turn to look surprised. "You thought I knew and was just looking for proof? Whom have you selected as the murderer?"

"Why, Tay, of course. I thought you had, too."

"Why Tay?"

Daphne looked vague. "I don't know. He isn't in the family, is he? I know Andrew thinks it was Tay. And you said the other night that someone had damaged the tyre in Uncle Hugh's car, the time they all went to Birmingham and I suppose it was the same person who killed him. Well, of course, that was Tay, wasn't it? So I don't see——"

I caught my breath. Burgess' voice was very quiet. "What makes you think it was Tay who damaged the tyre?"

"Well," said Daphne, still vaguely, "I just thought he did, that's all. That Sunday night we were all at dinner at Uncle Hugh's and I met Tay in the corridor. His hands were all dirty. He said something about having broken a flowerpot and that he was going to wash his hands. But when you talked about the tyre the other night, I thought you knew he had done it."

"Mrs. Alison," said Burgess, in a very sharp voice, "why didn't you tell me this before?"

Daphne jumped at his voice. She was evidently at the end of her endurance, for she broke into tears. Just then, there was a knock on the door and Robert burst in. He took one look around and said, "What the devil's going on in here?"

Daphne did not look up. Burgess said, "I've just been asking Mrs. Alison a few questions."

"I realize that. Was he bullying her, Chris?"

"He needed some information," I said, evasively. "Daphne's just a bit upset, that's all. The strain——"

"The strain of lying and keeping things to herself," said Robert, angrily. "What's come over you, Daphne? Why don't you tell me what all this is about and stop acting like the heroine of a second-rate melodrama?"

"Oh, let her alone, Robert," I said. "She——"

"I have let her alone," said Robert. "It hasn't done any good. I know damn well she didn't murder Uncle Hugh. But I also know she's been up to something else and I want to know what it is. I suppose if she can tell you and Burgess, she can tell me."

Robert was normally one of the most punctilious and polite young men, though he was not pompous. His behaviour showed how badly upset he had been by Daphne's performance during the strain of the last few days. But my cousin did not answer him. She did not even look up. And Robert, after a moment, turned and went out, banging the door behind him. Daphne did not move.

I began to think Robert was right in calling her behaviour suitable for second-rate melodrama. I got up. "Come on up to my room, Daphne," I said. "If you insist on crying, you can cry there in peace. If you stay here, your mother's likely to come barging in at any moment."

The possibility of having to face her mother had an effect on Daphne, and she followed me to my room without comment. Once there, she calmed down considerably. She went into the bathroom to wash her face, and came back to sit down quietly in a chair and light a cigarette. She smoked in silence for a moment or two. Then she said, in a normal voice, "You must think I'm a terrible fool."

"You've certainly given me some reason to think so during the last few days," I agreed.

To my surprise, she smiled a little. She shook her head. "I didn't mean that. I meant this affair with Phil. You *would* think it was silly if you knew all about it—the irresponsible, almost childish way I felt when I was with him, the kind of impossible plans we made. I think I knew they weren't possible even while we were making them. I couldn't go off to America with him, I couldn't leave the children— the whole thing was beyond me.

"You don't know what it meant to me, Chris—to have a part of my life separate and belonging to me and to no one else. No one knew about it. No one had a share in it. Nothing's ever been like that for me. My mother's always been there—watching me, planning for me, knowing everything I did. And my father wasn't far behind. And all the fuss about Andrew's future and Tay as a kind of shadow in the background.

"And all that talk—talk about the family and about Giles and Uncle Hugh and Charles and you. It was always going on. If I wasn't hearing about the family, it was politics—all the time. I hate politics, Chris. I don't understand it, it bores me. And all Robert's friends talk about it all the time. I've been so bored—for years now, it seems. Being with Phil was the most wonderful escape you can imagine."

It all came out as if she had been wanting to say it for a long time. I said, "But you wanted to marry Robert, didn't you?"

"Yes. I did. I've been happy with him, too. It's not that. But he's tied up with everything else in my life—with my family, with politics, with everything. Phil—don't you see, Chris?"

"Yes," I said.

I did see. I saw the instability I had always recognized in Daphne and about which Anne had commented. The whole thing was very complicated. If Daphne, desperately trying to find the money to pay her blackmailer, had thought wistfully of all the money she would have when Uncle Hugh died, it would not have been surprising. It was from there only a step to imagining the freedom of action she could have with money of her own; it would have made everything infinitely easier. She might then even have been able to get a divorce and to join Philip Denton in America, taking the children with her. It would probably have seemed an intoxicating future—much better than the rather dreary life divided between the political and business circles in which Robert moved and her own involved family.

I knew a little about Philip Denton. He was a writer, and a fairly good one. He was personable, lively, and above all, gay. Robert had his points and on the whole was probably a much better husband than Phil would be, but one could hardly have called him gay. Yes, I could see Daphne's position and she had a powerful motive for murder, a fact which I was certain Burgess had not overlooked.

But I somehow could not connect Daphne with the leakage of information at Uncle Hugh's plant. Daphne could have got the information and passed it on for money, and Uncle Hugh could have called her in Saturday night because he had discovered it— well, it was possible, but it seemed to me highly unlikely. Someone had to know or guess that Daphne needed money. Daphne had somehow to get access to the papers, assuming—a highly dubious assumption—that she would know them when she saw them. The only way she could see them would be if her father, her brother, Uncle Hugh, or Tay brought such papers home and left them lying around. No, it was too far-fetched. I just could not see it. If Daphne had in fact murdered Uncle Hugh, the trouble at the business could not be involved; and Burgess would have to look for two solutions instead of one.

After Daphne left me, I began to change for dinner. In the stress of the interview between Burgess and Daphne and my talk with Daphne afterwards, I had had no time to consider the other things that Burgess had learned that day: the telegram which Andrew had received and hidden; Tay's walking around with blackened hands the very evening the tyre had been damaged; Charles' early morning walk, the morning my uncle had been murdered and his link to the factory through his friend, Bryce. These were additional leads for Burgess, of course; but they seemed to point in so many different directions. I felt so tired and confused that it seemed the day had lasted for ever. I remembered with surprise that it had been only this morning that I had met the young man who wanted to form a Defence Committee for Giles. I decided that I would need more than one drink before dinner to make it possible for me to cope with the evening that lay ahead. But this was purely fatigue and strain; my newfound security was still with me, much as I dreaded what was yet to come.

Though it was early when I came down to the library, Charles was already there, having a drink. He gave me one. He said, "You've been spending a lot of time talking to Burgess to-day."

I could not tell what lay behind the question. "Yes," I said.

"He's an intelligent man," said Charles, musingly. "And he's gathered a lot of information. He's still gathering it, as a matter of fact. I just saw the gardener go in to talk to him—and I can't suppose it's to do with the way to grow roses or the best way to burn leaves. But I don't think Burgess has irrefutable proof yet—and that's what he needs. That leads me to believe he'll try shock tactics."

I could not tell whether he was probing for information or not. I said, "Well, he has to do something."

"Yes. But shock tactics can bring out a good many things that would be better left covered. The—what the sociologists call the fabric of family life, in our family, is sufficiently fragile anyway. I don't welcome the thought of its being made worse."

I said, curiously, "I didn't know the family weighed on you at all, Charles. Is all this because you now consider yourself its titular head?"

He shook his head. "I think it used to weigh on me a bit before the war, but during the war I more or less forgot it. It's years since I've spent this much time with them as a group and I've been thinking about it. I've begun to think my father has a good deal to answer for. Perhaps that's being unfair to him. He was a very strong man and he did as he pleased. But the fact that he was what he was made things difficult for many of his relatives. It might even have been the major factor in making them what they are."

"And you as well?"

"All of us," said Charles, evenly. "You, too, since we're being personal."

"Aunt Mildred?" I said, curiously. "Robert? Anne?"

"Aunt Mildred certainly—and even Robert and Anne a bit, though less so. And, speaking of Robert, what's the row between him and Daphne?"

I hesitated.

"Do give me credit for a little sense, Chris, even if some of the family are a little short on it. It's quite evident that Daphne's in a mess about something that has nothing to do with my father. Whether or not she murdered him is quite beside the point. And Daphne being what she is, it must have something to do with a man. She's been playing about?"

"Yes," I said. "And whether it has anything to do with Uncle Hugh's death I don't know, but it's quite possible."

Charles gave me an odd look. "And that's all you're going to say. All right. But remember what I told you, Christy. Don't get this thing out of proportion, even if you are acting as Burgess' right-hand man. One of us is most likely a murderer, but we aren't all therefore capable of committing murder. And by the way," he added, as we could hear some of the others coming down, "you're looking tired—but much better than you've looked for days."

I smiled. "You must have been watching me carefully."

"I have," said Charles. "I do."

His tone was entirely serious. I said, with some surprise, "Why?"

This time, Charles smiled. "You were always supposed to be very clever, Chris. You work it out for yourself."

The others came in then, and helped themselves to drinks. I retired with mine to a corner, and thought over my conversation with Charles. When I was talking to him, he seemed so reasonable that I could not believe he might be a murderer. Yet that proved nothing. When I talked to any of my relatives, they seemed—whatever their personal oddities—unlikely murderers.

We went in to dinner soon after the others came down. It was very good. Aunt Mildred remarked that no doubt the servants were making a special effort for the new owner and neither Daphne nor Robert seemed to enjoy themselves. But everyone else did, and Giles and Charles had an informed discussion about wine, in which—for a miracle—no one mentioned politics. When Charles spoke of a vine-yard he had visited in France, for instance, Giles did not discuss the antisocial, non-tax-paying habits of the French wine-growers. Instead, he listened civilly and added a few anecdotes of his own. It was the first time Burgess had seen Giles well behaved and my cousin's charm, so like Sir Hugh's, at its best. He must have been surprised.

The amiability and business-as-usual atmosphere of dinner was dissipated by my aunt as we sat in the drawing-room drinking coffee. She turned to Burgess and asked when we would be allowed to leave Feathers. "I have many things to attend to," she said. "And my husband

and my son are needed at the business. No doubt some of the others have their arrangements as well. If you cannot clear up this matter in a satisfactory way, I shall certainly write to the Home Secretary explaining our dissatisfaction with your conduct."

Burgess said courteously that he understood my aunt's impatience. He realized that we all must have plans and wish to be able to leave Feathers as soon as possible. "It's been a long day," he said, "and I don't believe a long session now would be the best plan. What I will do now, with your permission, is to tell you certain aspects of the case as I see them. Perhaps that will clear up a few things in everyone's mind. Then to-morrow morning, we can have a—final session."

Uncle William said, hoarsely, "Do you mean to say you know—who did it?"

"Let's say that I have certain ideas, Mr. Mason—and let it go at that for now. So, if you have no objections———"

If there were any, they were not voiced. Burgess began to speak, rather as if he were addressing a University seminar.

"This has been a very complicated case," he began. "And it became evident to me, in the course of my investigation, that almost everyone present stood to gain financially by this death. This was less important perhaps to some of you"—his eyes wandered around the room—"than to others. Some of you—Mrs. Mason and Mrs. Alison, especially—were in need of fairly large sums of money, which they very much preferred not to get from their husbands."

He raised his hand to forestall Uncle William's outburst. Robert made no attempt to speak. Burgess went on. "But money was by no means the only thing involved. A question of power was involved—control of the huge company Sir Hugh had built up. Mr. Tay and Mr. Andrew Mason were directly concerned in it. Both wanted control and both were tired of the struggle. They could perhaps not be blamed for feeling that, with Sir Hugh out of the way, things might—sort themselves out more readily. Nor were they the only ones involved in thinking about the control of the business. Mr. Charles Mason was interested as well, and kept in general touch with what was going on through a good friend of his, a man called Bryce, who works as a scientist in the laboratory."

Charles leaned forward as if about to speak, then sat back.

"Mr. William Mason was eager for his son to be the next chairman and willing to go to some lengths to achieve this—even to buying up some of the stock behind his brother's back. Mrs. Fane perhaps did not know any more than the rest of you that she would be in such an important position, as the result of her inheritance, but it is a fact worth bearing in mind."

No one moved, and no one spoke. Burgess had a clear field.

"We now come to another complication—Sir Hugh's interest in the Freemen of Britain. I believe that every member of this family was—to a greater or a lesser extent—opposed to Sir Hugh's connection with that organization. To put it at its simplest, any money given to the Freemen could not go to them. On a more complicated level, many of you disagreed with the aims of the Freemen. Perhaps the person most passionately opposed to Sir Hugh's activities on political grounds alone was Mr. Randall, who—as you all now know—threatened to murder Sir Hugh, should he judge it necessary."

It somehow sounded worse, in Burgess' dispassionate voice, than it had on the two previous occasions I had heard this threat mentioned.

"There is another point. Sir Hugh was, for various reasons, in possession of some information about certain members of his family that they might have preferred to keep hidden. So it is not impossible that he was murdered not directly for his money nor because anyone disapproved of his political activities, but rather because they hoped to prevent Sir Hugh from passing on that particular piece of information.

"I now come to what is in a way the least pleasant part of this investigation. It will probably be news to most of you that Sir Hugh was recently much troubled by the fact—I must ask all of you to refrain from mentioning this to anyone outside this room—that there had been a leakage of some important information from the scientific laboratory at his plant. Sir Hugh had reason to think"——Burgess ignored the universal gasp with which his announcement was greeted——"that this leak was possibly connected with someone high up in the organization or possibly connected with someone very closely related to himself. We may assume, I think, that anyone prepared to sell or to give secrets to——enemy powers——might well be willing to commit murder to keep this fact hidden."

By this time, everyone was beyond speech. Burgess rose. "Well, I think that is all I shall say right now. I shall be working in my bedroom until quite late. If there is anything anyone would like to tell me, I am of course available. If it should be something that I need to know, but that I need not make public to-morrow morning, it will certainly be to your advantage to tell me to-night."

We dispersed in stunned silence. I don't think anyone addressed a word to anyone else. When I got back to my room, I sat down in my chair for twenty minutes and did not move. I was too tired and too exhausted mentally and emotionally even to go to bed. Finally, I roused myself and looked around for a cigarette. After a few minutes' search, I realized with annoyance that I had left them downstairs. There was nothing to do but to go down and get them. There was a policeman on guard in the hall. He watched me stolidly, but made no move to stop me.

I found my cigarettes without any trouble and came up again. As I came back to go into my room, I glanced down the corridor. The policeman was looking, too. Charles was just turning the handle to Burgess' door. I hesitated for a moment on the threshold of my own room. Then I went in and went to bed. I fell asleep almost instantly.

XI

The next morning came soon enough. I felt heavy-headed and depressed, as—at Burgess' suggestion—we took our places around the dining-room table, now cleared of its breakfast things. Burgess was seated at the head and around it, in order, sat Anne, Daphne, Charles, Giles, myself, Tay, Robert, Aunt Mildred, Uncle William and Andrew.

"I am sorry," Burgess began, "that I did not get all the additional— co-operation—I hoped for last night. As a result, we may have to discuss some things rather openly, and it may prove rather embarrassing. But I'm sure you'd all welcome a quick solution to this—case." His pause was deliberate, meant to heighten the tension by reminding us all that, in spite of our position and the kid gloves which Burgess had had to use on this account, this was still an investigation for murder. His tactics succeeded, and the atmosphere around the table tautened.

"I think the simplest procedure," he went on, "would be to go over the events of that Saturday evening and night, from the time Mrs. Andrew Mason stopped in Sir Hugh's room, on her way down to dinner. You went in to see him, you said, Mrs. Mason, to ask him to dinner later in the month. But begin at the beginning. You knocked and he said come in. Is that right?"

"Yes," said Anne.

"Go on."

"Then he said, 'You look very nice, my dear,' and I said thank you. Then I said I'd come along to ask him to dine with us later in the month—and told him the names of the people who wanted to meet him. He said he thought it would be all right, and then we went down to the library together."

"He said he thought it would be all right. Did he look up the date in his diary?"

For the first time, I thought Anne hesitated. "No. He said he'd let me know later."

"Was this customary? I should have thought Sir Hugh was the kind of man who'd look up something like that immediately. He must have had a large number of engagements. Surely he'd look to see if the date was suitable."

"Well, he didn't," said Anne. "Perhaps he planned to do it the next morning and let me know definitely."

Charles intervened. "But that's very strange. It must have been the only time in his life he did such a thing. He *always* checked a date in his diary if he was asked to do something—he'd done it most of his life."

"Well," said Anne again, "he didn't this time."

Like Charles, I didn't entirely believe her. It was completely out of character for Uncle Hugh. But Burgess seemed inclined to let it go.

"Now after Mrs. Andrew Mason had gone down with Sir Hugh, I believe you went into Sir Hugh's room, Mrs. Mason." He turned to my Aunt Mildred. "What did you do there?"

My aunt was very stiff. "Mr. Burgess, I must protest. I consider this a most unseemly proceeding—bullying Anne, trying to bully the rest of us. I have no intention of answering any questions, and I would advise the rest of my family to refuse as well."

"Mrs. Mason," said Burgess, quietly, "we might digress for a moment. Let me ask you something. I believe you buy your clothes from a Madame Lebel."

My aunt looked surprised at the turn in the conversation. "Yes, I do—though I fail to see what that has to do with you."

"It has something," said Burgess. "I understand that recently you bought some expensive clothes there and that there was some unpleasantness about the bill."

Uncle William was looking angry, though I could not tell whether at Burgess or at his own wife.

"There was no unpleasantness," said my aunt. "They are always very reasonable about credit there. I am, after all, one of their best customers."

"Madame Lebel said she was uneasy about extending further credit to you, since there had been a large unpaid balance for nearly a year."

"She said nothing to me about that."

"Are you sure? Madame Lebel tells me there was another saleswoman present on that occasion."

My aunt showed some uneasiness. "Actually, I don't remember exactly what was said. I don't pay much attention to the ideas of tradespeople or to their remarks."

"Not even when they say they will not give you the clothes unless they receive substantial payment on account?"

"She didn't——" My aunt's eyes met those of Burgess, and she must have realized he knew what he was talking about. "She didn't put it exactly that way," she finished.

My uncle said, heatedly, "I fail to see what all this has to do with Hugh's death."

"It has this to do with it," said Burgess. "Mrs. Mason, I'm afraid you have not been quite candid. I am informed that in fact you were refused delivery of these new clothes without payment. However, you said that there was no need for the shop to worry as you would shortly be in possession of very large funds. According to Madame Lebel"—he looked down at the notes in front of him—"Mrs. Mason said that she expected a large access to her funds very soon and that she would be spending more on her clothes than heretofore. I knew of course that her brother-in-law was very rich and assumed either that he was about to make some new financial arrangements or else that he was ill and might not be expected to live long. I knew Sir Hugh had been in an accident and I thought he might have been more seriously hurt than had been announced. Mrs. Mason was one of our best customers, and she seemed so positive of getting additional money soon that I decided to risk it. You get to know pretty quickly in our business if people are telling the truth, and I thought Mrs. Mason was."

My uncle's face was very red, but no more so than his wife's. She started to speak several times, but it was a minute or more before she could control her voice. We must all have been looking at her curiously, and I saw on Charles' face the slight distaste which was almost always there when he spoke to my aunt.

"That lying woman!" she said. "It's a pity you don't investigate her and her black-market dealings instead of wasting our time here!"

"Unfortunately, that is not my province. This is. I repeat my question, Mrs. Mason. What did you mean when you said you expected a sudden access of funds?"

My aunt was normally not at all sensitive; but she could not remain unaware of the feeling in the room. "There's no point in your all looking at me," she burst out. "I haven't done anything. Clothes are expensive, and I've been a little short of money. I just said it to hold the woman off for a bit. I'd have paid her in the end, and she knew it. She doesn't give credit to people who won't."

"I see," said Burgess. "Madame Lebel also told me that she told you that if she didn't get her money within a month she would put the matter in the hands of her solicitor."

"She may have. I don't remember. But she certainly wouldn't have done such a thing."

"I'm also told, Mrs. Mason, that at one time, while you were discussing money matters with Madame Lebel, you referred to Sir Hugh. You said, 'He isn't particularly generous with money, my brother-in-law—when you consider that if it weren't for my husband, he wouldn't be where he is.'"

I wondered if my aunt's capacity to believe her own fantasies was so great that she had come to believe that. I expected her to deny this, too. But she didn't. She looked around the room and then, defiantly, at her husband. "All right," she said. "I did say it. What's more, I meant it. He wasn't generous with money—not really. He was never really generous with anything or with anyone. I never liked him. He thought he was God Almighty and other people just existed for his convenience. He never treated William as he deserved—or me—or Andrew."

She finally stopped. No one, not even Uncle William, was capable of speech after that outburst. But Burgess was. He said, "I'll now return to my original question, Mrs. Mason. What did you do in Sir Hugh's room?"

My aunt was beaten, and she knew it. "Nothing," she said, dully. "I looked at some papers on his desk, but they didn't mean anything to me—they were letters to constituents or something like that. I only stayed a minute or two. Then I went downstairs."

"Well, that's clear," said Burgess. "After that, you all had drinks in the library and no one went upstairs again until Mrs. Fane did, at about 9.30."

Everyone agreed. Burgess said to me, "How long were you upstairs?"

"About ten minutes."

"What did you do?"

"I just looked in the rooms, to make sure they'd been made ready for the night."

"Did you go into them?"

"No."

"Just opened the doors and looked in?"

"That's right."

"And that took ten minutes?"

"It—well, no. I went into my own room for a couple of minutes."

Everyone stirred. I remembered that I had not said this before.

"What did you do in your room?"

"Nothing much. I got a clean handkerchief and I put on some lipstick."

"And that's all?"

"Yes. Then I came downstairs."

"And after that, no one went upstairs until the party began to break up, about eleven?" Burgess consulted his notes. "You went up first, didn't you, Mrs. Mason?"

"Yes," said Anne.

"Do anything special?"

"No," said Anne. "I just went up and went to bed."

"Right," said Burgess. "Then the rest of you went up, more or less at the same time. You went into his room with your brother, didn't you, Mr. Mason?"

"I did," said Uncle William, and folded his lips back. He was clearly planning to say nothing more.

"Did you go in to discuss with him your transactions with Mr. Cotton?"

My uncle turned very red. He did not answer. Burgess said, "What puzzles me is what you hoped to accomplish by having Mr. Cotton buy up any outstanding shares in the company and hold them for you in his name. You surely couldn't get control of the company that way!"

Tay and Andrew looked baffled. But Charles said, "I don't think he was planning to get control of the company. He knew enough to know it couldn't be done—there weren't enough shares in outside hands to be bought. I'd guess he wanted to accumulate as many voting shares as he could, on the quiet—and use them for nuisance value—to persuade my father to pay more attention to him than he'd ever done."

"And why not?" said my Uncle William. His voice was very bitter. "And why not? I'd been with the company almost as long as he had. I knew as much about it. And he paid almost no attention to me. He let an outsider"—he gave Tay a look of infinite loathing—"he let an outsider get in a controlling position and he ignored me. I had a right to be heard. If I took some method to try to bring myself into a better position to have my advice followed, I don't see anything wrong with that."

"But your brother might have," said Burgess. "Suppose he disliked the idea of what you were doing—behind his back. Perhaps he was going to remove you from your position in the company altogether. In that case, the temptation to remove him before he could remove you must have been very great."

"That's not so," said my uncle. "Hugh didn't give a damn. He——" He stopped.

"Then he knew," said Burgess. "Was that the subject you had to discuss with him so urgently Saturday night?"

Uncle William looked around the room in search of a way out of the trap into which he had blundered. "No," he said, angrily. "I had to discuss a small point about the business."

"Then Sir Hugh told you at that time that he knew of your activities?"

If Uncle William had been a quick thinker, he would have said yes. For if Uncle William had learned at 11.15 that night that his brother resented his activities and planned to remove him from the company, he would hardly have been able to put the drug into Sir Hugh's carafe there and then. But Uncle William was not quick-witted, and he rose to the bait. "He did *not* tell me for the first time then. He told me earlier in the week."

"Just so," said Burgess. The point was obvious, and he left it. He said to Tay, "Then you were the next person to visit Sir Hugh. I believe Mr. Mason met you as he was coming out of Sir Hugh's room."

"That's right," said Tay. "I also had a small point I wanted to take up with him. I wasn't there very long."

"You didn't talk with him about the Freemen?"

"No. Not then. I had talked to him about it, though."

"Telling him you thought it was a bad idea?"

"Just that." Tay smiled faintly. "I hadn't convinced him."

"Mr. Tay, when I mentioned last night that there had been espionage at the plant, you were surprised?"

"Stunned would be more accurate, Inspector. Yes. I was. But I didn't share your conclusion."

"No?" Burgess was very polite.

"No. I'm inclined to believe that it must have been one of the scientists. That's the sort of thing that's been happening, isn't it? And anything else appears unthinkable."

"Of course, you may be right. But I should prefer to leave that until later. I want to go back a bit—to the motor-car crash. You were very sure, the other night, that I could learn very little more about that, weren't you?"

"I didn't see how. *Have* you learned more about it?"

"Perhaps. I've learned at least that you were seen that night, wandering about Sir Hugh's house, with very dirty hands. It's a curious thing to have at a dinner-party. Would you care to explain?"

Tay was a little pale, but he smiled again, faintly. "Circumstantial evidence?" he asked. "It's very simple. I went into the conservatory and by accident I broke a flowerpot. I tried to pick up some of the pieces and got my hands filthy. You can ask the servants—they'll tell you. I don't imagine they were too pleased."

Burgess did not smile. "You're a very clever man, Mr. Tay. I don't doubt you broke the flowerpot—that's just what you *would* do to give yourself a reasonable excuse for having dirty hands when you hadn't been doing anything more strenuous than drinking coffee."

"Perhaps I would have," said Tay, "had I in fact damaged that tyre. But I didn't. And you can't prove I did."

"Possibly not, Mr. Tay. We'll see about that." He was about to go on, but my Aunt Mildred interrupted him.

"Well, aren't you going to arrest him?" she demanded, shrilly. "You sit here badgering all of us with insolent questions that have nothing to do with the murder, and all the time the murderer's as plain as a pikestaff. What are you waiting for?"

"All in good time, Mrs. Mason. We have a way to go yet." Burgess' quiet, authoritative voice silenced my aunt, and she sat back again. But every time she glanced at Tay, there was a look of vindictive triumph on her face.

I felt a little sick. What Burgess was trying to do was evident. He was using the same tactics as he had the other night—hoping to arouse us to such a pitch of tension that we would lose control and say things we might otherwise not have done: hoping in this way to trap a murderer. I thought of what Charles had said about the delicate fabric of our family life. It certainly looked ugly enough just now.

Burgess was proceeding like a time-table. "Then you arrived, Mr. Mason. And what did you do?"

"Paid the car," said Charles, succinctly. "Went upstairs. Knocked at the door of my father's room. He told me to come in. I did. He asked how I had happened to come over that night, and I explained. Then——"

"Just one moment, Mr. Mason. You explained what?"

"I explained that I had been made uneasy by certain of the rumours I had heard in connection with him and the Freemen. We talked about it for a bit and I tried to dissuade him from doing anything public about the organization—announcing his support or anything like that. But though he said we'd talk about it, his mind was made up. So I went to bed."

"Well, but did you, Mr. Mason?"

"Did I what?"

"Did you go to bed?"

"Of course."

"And you didn't go out again?"

Everyone was sitting up very straight and some of us were leaning forward. The room seemed very close, as if there were no air—though the windows were open. Charles looked at Burgess for a moment and then smiled. I could have sworn the amusement was genuine. He said, "Of course. I forgot. I went for a walk."

Someone gasped. Burgess was unmoved. "You went to bed, got up, went for a walk, and then undressed again and went to bed?"

"No." My cousin hesitated. "I couldn't sleep—I wasn't very tired. I just sat in my room and read. About—just before five, it must have been—I decided to get some air. I felt restless. So I went outside and walked around the garden. Then it began to rain and I came in again. That was when I got undressed and went to bed."

"You weren't tired, even though you'd been working hard in Paris and had flown over late at night?"

"Perhaps I was over-tired and had got over being sleepy."

"So you sat in your room and read? Perhaps you thought over your conversation with your father?"

"I may have done."

"You were passionately against your father's publicly allying himself with the Freemen?"

"As I've told you, I was against his having anything to do with them at all."

"It would have been very much contrary to your interests if he had continued to associate with them?"

"I'm not certain what you mean by that. It wouldn't have affected me directly. The Foreign Office usually doesn't hold one responsible for the sins of one's parents. But I disagreed with what he—with what they were trying to do."

"But financially, you might have suffered."

"No, not particularly."

"I've been checking into your activities in Paris a bit, Mr, Mason. You're known to be extravagant and to live on a high standard. If your father had given large sums to the Freemen—as he seems to have been planning to do—he might have given you less, especially since he knew you to be so much out of sympathy with him about the organization."

"You can think that," said Charles, "only because you didn't know my father. He didn't react like that."

"You understood him so well?"

"I knew what he was likely to do under certain circumstances."

"Did his support of the Freemen fit into your conception of him?"

"Not at first. But when I talked to him, I saw how he'd been thinking lately, and then it seemed in character."

"So you could be mistaken in your analysis of him on other points?"

"It's possible. But I don't think I was."

Burgess looked unconvinced. "I've another suggestion to offer about your behaviour that night, Mr. Mason. Let's look at it this way. You learn in Paris that your father is likely to make a public announcement of a project of which you disapprove. More, you have reason to think it might eventually work out very much against your own interests. You come home at considerable inconvenience to yourself and to other people, and you go in to see your father. He confirms your suspicions of the way he is going to act. You are prepared for this, and you put the drug into his carafe. You then return to your own room—and it's not surprising, if my analysis is correct, that you can't sleep. I couldn't either. About five o'clock, or just before, you look into his room to see if he's dead. He is. You are at once upset by what you've done and delighted at your success. You go for a walk. Then you come back and go to bed quietly. When the maid comes to you the next morning with the news, you are able to simulate all the proper reactions—you've had plenty of time to prepare yourself. What have you to say to that?"

The room was deathly quiet. "Only that there's not a word of truth in it," said Charles.

"I've another point, Mr. Mason. Your very good friend, Edward Bryce, worked in the laboratory at your father's plant. I believe you were influential in getting him the job. In return, he sent you reports on things at the plant from time to time. Why? And did he send you anything else?"

The tension in the room was almost unbearable. Charles said, "I got Edward the job because he was a good scientist and my father's plant was a good place to work. We've always corresponded from time to time—except during the war. Besides being a scientist, Edward's very intelligent. He didn't like my father's interest in the Freemen, of which he'd heard something, and he'd thought for some time that the rivalry between Andrew and Tay was bad for morale. I thought he exaggerated its effects—but, of course, I was interested. I'd have spoken to my father about it, if I'd come to think it as serious as he did. As to his sending me anything else—I cannot imagine that you meant that question seriously. Among other things, I was, as you know, an Intelligence Officer. That's the sort of thing I know about. To put it at its crudest, do you think I'd have arranged for a leakage with such an obvious connection pointing directly at me?"

"A very clever man might, Mr. Mason." The eyes of the two men met. It was for the time being a duel between the two of them, with the rest of us excluded. "And I've still another point. Everyone has agreed that no one knew the contents of Sir Hugh's will. This may or may not be true. But I've thought all along that the most likely person to know anything about it was you. To whom does a man confide things, if not to his only son? You stood to gain more by the will than anyone else—more money and more power. If you knew the contents of the will, you knew you could control the company. You hold 25 per cent of the voting shares. With those, you could pretty well dictate either to Mr. Tay or to your cousin Andrew. In fact, you could probably persuade your cousin, Mrs. Fane, to vote your way whatever you did—even if you wanted to run the company yourself."

My cousin's voice was still steady. "That may all have been possible. But it's not true."

"No?" said Burgess. "Then tell me this, Mr. Mason. When the will was read, I was watching your face. You flushed to the roots of your hair. It's the only time I've seen your composure shaken—until now, of course. Why? Was it because you realized it was all yours now—all that money, all that power? Was that it, Mr. Mason?"

"No," said Charles. For the first time, I noted that his composure had been shaken. "No. That wasn't it. You want to know what it was. I'll tell you. It wasn't what you think at all. I'd been hearing for years—ever since I was a small boy and not just from my family—that I wasn't the son my father wanted—that he'd always wanted me different. When that will was read, I knew it wasn't so—that he'd been entirely satisfied with me all along. I don't know why, I didn't think I cared about it—but when I learned that, it moved me. And that's why I flushed. That's all there was to it. I did not murder my father. I couldn't have murdered my father. I understood him too well. I disapproved of his association with the Freemen, yes. I disapproved of a lot of other things he did. But I didn't murder him!"

I had never in my life heard Charles talk like that. To me, at least, it sounded convincing. But Burgess was not so sure. "It's an explanation," he said. "I'm afraid it's not one I can easily accept. Let me put it this way. You had the opportunity to put the drug in your father's carafe. You stood to gain a good deal by his death. On your morning walk, you had the opportunity to get rid of any incriminating evidence you might have left. And against this unusual behaviour, we have only your word?"

"That's right," said Charles. His emotion had gone and he was as calm as he normally was. I waited with apprehension for Burgess' next words. They could easily be, "I'm afraid I'll have to take you into custody, Mr. Mason."

But they were not. Instead, the Inspector said, in a pleasant, almost conversational voice, "Of course, much of what I said to you, Mr. Mason, applies to almost everyone else at this table as well."

This long, drawn-out inquisition was beginning to have its effects. Everyone round the table looked as if they had been through a difficult ordeal.

"Well," said Burgess, still in his conversational voice, "that brings us to just before midnight. Mrs. Alison, I believe you went to see your uncle next."

"Yes," said Daphne. Her voice was so quiet that it was difficult to hear it.

"To ask him for money?"

"Yes."

"Did he give it to you?"

"No."

"Had you asked him for it before?"

"Oh, no," said Daphne. She sounded surprised.

"But you'd needed it for some time?"

"I—yes."

"For how long?" asked Burgess, relentlessly.

"About two months."

"A long time. Whatever you needed it for—must have been becoming urgent."

Daphne made no reply. "Was it, Mrs. Alison? Was it becoming urgent?"

Daphne only nodded. She seemed unable to speak.

"Your uncle's death would have given you all the money you needed?"

Daphne nodded again. She seemed hypnotized.

"People like you, Mrs. Alison," said Burgess, still in his easy voice, "are the kind that panic and do foolish things—like committing murders that can be traced to them."

Daphne, I thought? *Daphne?* But Burgess was looking down at his notes again, and beginning to turn his questions to Andrew. I glanced at Robert. He was looking at his wife in the same cold, impersonal way he had done for the last few days. But I thought I noticed a slight change on his face. It looked like compassion.

"Then you went along to see Sir Hugh, Mr. Mason. You didn't meet your sister?"

"No," said Andrew.

"And you went to talk to him about the Freemen?"

"That's right."

Burgess selected a yellow paper from the pile in front of him. "I've a telegram of yours here, Mr. Mason. Perhaps you'd like to explain it."

Andrew took it and read it through twice. He frowned. He handed it back to Burgess. He said, "I've never seen it before."

Either my cousin was a wonderful actor or else he was telling the truth. His voice sounded entirely sincere. Burgess said, "It's addressed to you."

"Yes. But I've never seen it."

"Do you understand what it means?"

Andrew hesitated. But that morning had given him a taste of Burgess' quality. "Yes."

"So do I," said Burgess. "But suppose you explain it anyway. Perhaps I'd better read it. It says, 'George tricky stop Suggest Peter Able.'"

Andrew said, emotionlessly, "It's from an—acquaintance of mine. 'George tricky' simply meant he had definite information Uncle Hugh was going to throw in his lot openly with the Freemen."

"Your friend, of course, is a private detective?"

By now, everyone was looking at Andrew in consternation. My cousin said, "Yes."

"Whom you were paying to spy on your uncle?"

"If you care to put it that way. As I've told you, I thought my uncle's activities were ill-considered. I thought it important to know what he was planning to do. Apparently this detective picked up something which made him certain of my uncle's plans. He couldn't very well write me here in detail—or perhaps he just hadn't the time. Anyway, he seems to have sent that wire. But, as I say, I never got it."

"We'll go into that in a minute, if you don't mind, Mr. Mason. Let's finish with the telegram. What does 'Peter Able' mean?"

For the first time, Andrew looked a little uneasy. "It means—plan one." He began to speak more quickly. "I had never mentioned the matter to my uncle—I'd put off doing it till I was sure. Plan one was just talking to my uncle—it was my last resort."

"You talked to your uncle that night, after you got the telegram?"

"I never got it," repeated Andrew. "I did talk to him, yes. I told you that. The reason I did was because he had Gresham here. I'd worked out easily enough that Gresham was connected with the Freemen—it couldn't have been anything else. So I decided to have a word with my uncle anyway."

"You're an ingenious family," said Burgess. "I've seldom heard so many interesting explanations of things which seem to me to have simpler but more damning explanations. I'll offer you a different explanation, Mr. Mason. I suggest that you did in fact get the telegram, and decided to act; and that Plan One was not a simple chat with your uncle but something much less innocent—the murder of your uncle."

Andrew was pale. "You can suggest it. But it is not true."

"I shan't bore everyone here with your motive. It's obvious. To control a company like that—which you may well have thought you would at your uncle's death—would be a temptation to any ambitious man. And you're an ambitious man, Mr. Mason. Means, motive, opportunity—and this telegram. It all fits, doesn't it?"

"Too many things fit," said Andrew, his face still taut. "But it's not true. Furthermore, I never got that telegram. And I'd like to know who did."

"You received it yourself, Mr. Mason. I've questioned the staff and none of them remember seeing it. And as you've probably noticed, it's addressed to you here."

The telegram was lying on the table. More to avoid looking at anyone's face than anything else, I picked it up. I said, "It came Saturday afternoon, didn't it? That was the one time Raikes might have been in the house. Have you asked him?"

To everyone's astonishment, Tay said in a voice which sounded almost bored, "You needn't bother to ask him. I took the telegram. Raikes gave it to me and I said I'd give it to Andrew."

There was a collective gasp. Andrew looked at Burgess triumphantly, and Burgess looked just slightly taken aback. It was his first slip. It was not big enough to loosen his hold on all of us. He had been too tough for that. But he could not keep his dominance if he made many more.

He said, "I'm sorry, Mr. Mason. But you must realize that it changes nothing. You yourself told me that when you said you'd guessed Gresham's errand here."

"It proves I was telling the truth on that point at least," said Andrew. "And I say again I've told the truth all along. But what about Tay?" There was an ugly look on his face. "Funny how everything seems to come back to Tay—beginning with the tyre. And what about that information leakage at the plant? Tay was in a good spot for it. And if Uncle Hugh found out——"

I had never seen Andrew display his hate for Tay so openly before. I reflected dully, for the second time that morning, that the fabric of our ordinary relationships was certainly being torn savagely. Burgess said to Tay, "I think you'd better explain, Mr. Tay."

Tay was looking entirely self-possessed, but very sad. He said, "Frankly, I hoped the matter of the telegram wouldn't come up at all. I didn't see that it made any difference to the case. But I was afraid you wouldn't see it that way."

I could not imagine what he meant. Neither could Burgess, apparently. He waited for further explanation.

"You see," said Tay, "the telegram arrived Saturday afternoon. Raikes was in a hurry to get back to the garage, so I took the telegram and said I would give it to Andrew. I put it in my pocket—and forgot all about it. The next day, after Sir Hugh's death, I found it still in my pocket. I opened it and read it. I didn't understand it, but I could see that it might—divert anyone looking for a murderer. I didn't want that to happen, and I didn't want Andrew to come under any unnecessary suspicion. So I hid it away in what I assumed would be a safe place, and I thought I'd give it to Andrew when everything had been settled."

Burgess was as incredulous at this as the rest of us. "I am to understand that the object of your unusual behaviour was to save Mr. Mason from coming under unnecessary suspicion?"

"Yes."

"You did this in spite of the state of relations between the two of you?"

"Yes."

"You ask me to believe that you went out of your way, even to the point of causing yourself to be under additional suspicion, in order to protect Mr. Mason?"

Tay smiled faintly. He looked very weary. "It's quite true. You see, I've never had any doubt of the murderer—not from the moment I heard that Sir Hugh had been killed. There was only one possible murderer—if one knew everyone involved. Of course, you didn't. That was precisely the difficulty. That's why I took what you evidently consider an extraordinary step in order to keep you from wasting your time suspecting Andrew."

The tension in the room was at that point almost unbearable. "You have always been quite sure of the identity of the murderer, have you?" asked Burgess, softly. "Perhaps you'd tell me whom you have in mind?"

"Certainly. The only person who could have murdered Sir Hugh is his nephew, Giles Randall."

Giles half-rose in his seat, and sat back again. Aunt Mildred had a curious little look of triumph on her face. Andrew merely looked puzzled. And Burgess waited, as we all did. Tay went on quietly:

"Giles has always hated Sir Hugh. The fact that his uncle was generous to him seems to have made him hate him the more. He was obsessed with his uncle. It wasn't just ordinary, straightforward hatred. He couldn't leave him alone, couldn't stop thinking about him. D'you suppose he'd have spent all that time ferreting out Sir Hugh's activities if he'd just disliked his uncle? Of course not. Sir Hugh knew about it. He said to me, more than once, ' I don't know what's bothering that boy, but sometimes I think he'll murder me.' That very Saturday night, he threatened his uncle. What other reason had he to come sneaking into the house after midnight? No, I always knew it was

Giles. But I was afraid you'd get misled by some irrelevant details and miss the main point."

No one spoke for a moment. It was evident that Tay believed what he was saying. Burgess said, "Can you explain also your rather surprising desire to protect Mr. Andrew Mason?"

Tay again gave his weary smile. "Of course Andrew and I have been rivals for control of the company. That's no secret. I'd do anything I could to defeat him—in a business way. But men don't murder for the control of a business. I wouldn't. Andrew wouldn't. Men who murder are fanatics—like Giles."

He leaned forward. "I don't know whether you understand what people like Giles are after. I do—and I'll fight it with everything in me. He wants to level everything off—everything but the gains possible for the few people on top. No one will own anything but their clothes and a few household possessions. Everything else—houses, anything—will be held on temporary lease from the State. He hates the kind of living the few who wanted it have been able to enjoy. He'll destroy it if he can. His uncle understood him very well. I don't agree with the method Sir Hugh selected with which to fight. But I can see why he chose it. You say why did I protect Andrew, whom you assume to be my enemy. Andrew is my rival in the control of the *Company*. That's all. If he should win and I should lose, I might be out of a controlling position. But my kind of life and my kind of world would remain. Giles wants to kill that kind of world. And you ask me why I'd try to protect Andrew."

Giles would be silent no longer. "Your kind of life!" he said. "Your kind of world! My Uncle Hugh was only possible in *your* kind of world—my Uncle Hugh and the kind of control he could have over millions of people. Look what he's done to people! Look what he's done to his own family! Destroy that kind of world? Of course I would. I'd count it a privilege!"

"Perhaps you did destroy a part of it, Mr. Randall," said Burgess. His voice was silky. "At least, that part of it represented by Sir Hugh.

We might talk about that for a moment. This friend of yours—the one you're staying with—Miss Bella Moore, isn't it?"

"Yes," said Giles.

"Were you aware, Mr. Randall, that Miss Moore suffers from high blood-pressure?"

I held my breath.

Giles said, coolly, "Bella imagines things."

"She may well do. But in this case she's not imagining it. She does suffer from high blood-pressure. Her doctor is treating her for it. The drug, Mr. Randall, which she is taking is called hexamethonium bromide. By a curious coincidence, it's exactly the same drug which was used to kill your uncle. I told you that, do you remember? And you said vaguely that you thought you'd heard of it. Since Miss Moore keeps a regular supply of it, you must have been reasonably well informed about it. Yet you gave me a deliberately vague reply when I mentioned it to you. Why?"

"No particular reason," said Giles, sulkily. "I didn't see that it mattered."

"It mattered very much indeed," said Burgess. There was now an edge on his voice. "But there's more to it, Mr. Randall. This morning your friend, Miss Moore—whom we've been watching with some care—was found trying to dispose of a small bottle that had contained tablets. Clumsy of her, all things considered. I don't need to tell you what the bottle had contained."

"What?" asked Giles, hoarsely.

"Hexamethonium bromide."

Through the conflicting voices, the next clear one I could hear was Burgess'. He said, "Can you give me one reason, Mr. Randall, why I should not arrest you for the murder of your uncle, Sir Hugh Mason?"

Giles' face was white. The tension in the room seemed at the breaking-point. But Giles managed to speak. He said, quietly, "Yes: the best reason. I didn't do it."

"Well," said Burgess, "let's look at it. Of all those who had the opportunity to kill him, you disliked him the most. You were overheard threatening to kill him. You had easy access to the drug—which you tried, rather unintelligently, to conceal. You either contrived in some way to let Miss Moore know which drug was used—you told me you hadn't known till I gave you the information—or else you really did know all along and lied to me."

"I didn't know," said Giles, with great effort. "The village gossip was confusing. But from what they said, I guessed. When I spoke to Bella over the telephone, I hinted at it to her. She must have understood. I don't know why she tried to get rid of the bottle. It was a silly thing to do. I certainly didn't tell her to do it."

"It's probably because she thinks you're guilty, Mr. Randall. She's said you've been unlike yourself since your uncle's death—upset and confused. Considering your sentiments about your uncle, I can scarcely put those symptoms down to grief!"

Giles did not reply.

Tay said, "*And* he's the one who's most likely to be tied up with that information leak at the plant. Charles knew a scientist—well, you'll probably find Giles knows one, too. It's the sort of thing he would do—because of his political beliefs and because he thought it a way to damage Sir Hugh. That's why Sir Hugh didn't tell me—or Andrew. He was appalled to think he had a nephew who could be a traitor!"

There were two red spots on Giles' cheek-bones. He looked like someone driven into a corner. When he spoke, his voice sounded very queer—not like his own at all. "A traitor?" he repeated. "It's you who are traitors—you and Sir Hugh and the lot of you—who'd exploit your own countrymen and sell them to the Americans sooner than give up your own miserable profits. But one of the troubles is that you're not very bright, are you? *I'm* not a Communist. I never have been. I don't give secrets away—not to the Russians or to anyone else. If you knew anything about me at all, you'd know that. But"—he almost smiled, except that it was more a baring of the teeth than a smile—"you've got a Communist among you all right. So if you're looking for who gave away the secrets, you don't have to look much further. Do they Anne?"

The very walls seemed to move toward us, and to make the room like a torture-chamber. I heard my own involuntary exclamation, and I heard Andrew say, "It's a filthy lie!" and heard the scraping of his chair as he pushed it back. But Robert reached across the table to shove him back in his chair, and Charles said, "Why don't you let your wife answer that, Andrew?"

Anne was looking at us all—and clearly finding our horror a little strange, almost out of place and in questionable taste. Her voice, when she spoke, was chilly and remote. "I won't trouble to deny it," she said. "It's only a matter of time. Sir Hugh had it all written down somewhere—he told me so that night when I went in to see him before dinner. I believe he was going to square it with the authorities in some way—at least, fix it so it wouldn't get out. What other steps he planned to take, I don't know. I——"

Andrew interrupted her. His voice was hoarse. "Anne, you don't mean it. You can't! It means you'd have got the information from me—those papers I brought home——"

Anne looked at him thoughtfully. "Of course that's where I got it. I didn't think it would be discovered so soon—and given a little time, we could have covered our tracks. But they—the Party, I mean—seemed to think the information was important. I'm sorry you feel badly about it, Andrew, and that you had to be involved like this. But there isn't anything personal in it. I'm very fond of you, I always have been. It's only that this—is so much more important."

No one could think of an adequate answer—or any answer at all. It would have been like arguing with a robot—or a tank. I felt as if I were going to be sick, but Charles put his hand on mine and it seemed to steady me a little. Finally, Burgess said, "Did Sir Hugh tell you, Mrs. Mason, that he was going to tell Andrew the next day—after the lunch? And that Andrew would, of course, divorce you? Is that why you killed him?"

Anne looked surprised. "But I didn't kill him. Surely Giles did."

"You went up first—ahead of everyone else. You had a chance to go into his room then."

"I went up only a minute or so before Sir Hugh came up with—my father-in-law. He can tell you that."

Uncle William shot her a glance of loathing. But she had evidently told the truth, for he did not deny it. I thought two—two people—two people like that—among us, and I again thought I could stand it no longer. Then I looked again at Anne's face, entirely calm, entirely sure of herself, and I braced myself. If she could stand being what she was, I could stand learning about it.

After the pause, Anne repeated, "But Giles? What about Giles?" There was some slight feeling in her voice for the first time. I had not realized until then that she hated him.

Burgess seemed to come back from a long way. He looked around the table slowly. "Yes, Mr. Randall. What about you?" He looked down at his notes, and then up again with a new access of decision. "I've been struck all along by one thing. It's been generally agreed by everyone that Sir Hugh was in buoyant spirits that evening. You, of course, didn't know that as you weren't here. You told me that he seemed if anything quieter and more subdued than usual. Doesn't it strike you as significant that your description of him differs from that of everyone else who saw him that night?"

"I don't see what that proves," said Giles. The episode with Anne seemed in some way to have restored him. He looked intolerably strained, but more in control of himself than he had ten minutes earlier.

"It suggests that you lied on that point," said Burgess. "Or perhaps you didn't actually lie. Perhaps you were so taken up with your plans for murdering him and with putting the tablets into his carafe that you didn't notice how he was behaving."

"That's not true," said Giles. "I did notice, and it was exactly as I told you. He did seem quieter. I can't help it if the others found him lively. After all, it was very late when I saw him. Maybe he was tired."

When Daphne spoke, her voice seemed to come from far away—almost as if it were someone else, not herself, speaking. "Of course, he had a headache, didn't he? Do you suppose that might account for it?"

All heads turned towards her as if on a swivel. Burgess said in a sharp voice, "He had a headache? How do you know?"

Daphne blinked. "Why, he said so. Does it matter?"

"Why didn't you tell me that before?"

"I didn't think of it. It slipped my mind. But just now, when Giles said he seemed a bit subdued, I remembered it."

Burgess said, evenly, "Did he say anything else?"

"Anything else?" My cousin sounded almost half-witted.

Burgess said, patiently, "Did your uncle ever take anything when he had a headache?"

"Did he—oh, I see. Why, yes. He took aspirin, like anyone else. As a matter of fact, you're right. He said he had a slight headache, and he was just taking some aspirin when I came in."

Burgess looked at Daphne in silence for a moment. He took a deep breath. He sat very still a moment longer. Then he said, gently, "All right. Now let's see if we can't tie things up. A couple of aspirin," he said, almost to himself. "Now a couple of aspirin would hardly have a seriously depressing effect on a man—not enough to make him feel cold and seem markedly less lively than normal. And this would seem to argue"—his voice was very quiet—"this would seem to argue that it's possible that by the time Mr. Randall saw his uncle, Sir Hugh had already taken the hexamethonium bromide. On the other hand, the doctors tell me that the drug would have taken about two hours to work. Therefore, if it had already been in the water when Mrs. Alison saw him take the aspirin—which must have been just past midnight—he would have been dead by two o'clock. And at that time, according to Gresham, he was alive enough to turn out his light. So we can place the time the drug was put into the carafe a bit more exactly, can't we?"

No one seemed to breathe. It was as if a judge were pronouncing sentence.

Burgess opened an envelope which had been among his notes, and extracted a soiled handkerchief. It had blood on it, and some black marks that did not look like ordinary dirt. He said to Giles, "Is this yours?"

Giles, puzzled, shook his head. Robert, who had not yet put two and two together, said in a rather surprised voice, "Why, it's yours, isn't it, Andrew? You threw it away after you cut your hand. You remember—Sunday morning."

"Of course you threw it away, Mr. Mason," said Burgess. "No doubt you deliberately cut your hand, so you could have an excuse to throw the handkerchief away. And in the normal course of events the handkerchief *would* have been burned. But things didn't go normally. The gardener's little girl found it. She liked the blood on it—children do. She kept it. She didn't even play with it—just put it away. I suppose she was afraid the blood would wear off if she played with it. When the gardener found it yesterday, he brought it to me. I've looked at it with some care, as you can imagine. I even had some other people look at it, to make sure. This black is silver polish, and this handkerchief's clearly been used to wipe off some silver polish. I take it, Mr. Mason, that you've been cleaning your silver cigarette-case?"

My aunt's voice cut in, impatient and malicious. "There's another mistake, Mr. Burgess. My son doesn't like anything silver. He doesn't own a silver cigarette-case."

XII

"I see," said Burgess. "I've seen for some time. Well, Mr. Mason?"

Andrew looked at us all for a few seconds without speaking. It was only too evident that we all saw—all except Aunt Mildred, of course. It was also evident that he no longer cared. Anne's revelation must have been the final straw. When he spoke, it was in a quiet, resigned, relaxed, placid voice.

"I do not wish to argue," he said. "Sometimes I've thought, from the things you've said, that you knew all along, and were only waiting for a suitable moment. The ironical thing is that you never had the right reason. You don't see it now. You thought it was *because* I wanted control of the business. I did want that. But I could have waited—if my uncle had been going along in the ordinary way, that is. But he wasn't. Do you know what his association with the Freemen would have done to the company? It would have ruined it—ruined it—and you were all too stupid to see it. Well, I wasn't. I saw it plainly enough. I knew what it would mean. If he'd gone on as he meant to do, there wouldn't have been any business for me to run even if I finally did get control. That motor-car accident would have solved everything—if it had worked—but it didn't. I'd lived for that business. I never remember really thinking of anything else. My family"—he slowly and placidly surveyed his parents, and I could not tell what was in that look; he did not look at his wife—"my family never talked of anything else. 'Andrew'll run the business. Uncle Hugh would be lost without Andrew. You've got to be even better than Uncle Hugh!' I never cared about anything else, not really, and he was going to ruin it. So I killed him!"

We sat frozen under the quiet spell of words. Then Andrew broke from the room and ran upstairs. Burgess pursued, but he was too late. Andrew gained his own room and locked the door. By the time they had forced it open, Andrew was dead.

XIII

They did not stay long at Feathers after that. My Uncle William took his wife away. I did not go to say good-bye to them. I knew they would not want to see me. Robert, his essential gentleness and decency coming out as I would have expected, took Daphne home. She had completely broken down. Charles called Lord Durcott, who came to Feathers for Anne. She did not talk to any of us—just shut herself up in Charles' room and remained there quite alone. When her father called for her, she went with him without having said a word to a soul. Charles and Tay, with Burgess' help, drafted a statement for the press. It was as tactful as could be expected, and made no mention of Anne and the information leakage. Burgess and Charles and MI5 settled that somehow among them. Giles went off to Redcot and Bella, and, as I learned later, returned to London that very night.

Burgess told us later that he had been almost certain Andrew was guilty of the murder from the moment he had been given my cousin's discarded handkerchief. He had hoped to bring him to the breaking-point by producing the telegram. When that had failed, he had decided to try confronting Andrew with the handkerchief anyway. Daphne's sudden recollection about the aspirin had made Burgess' case watertight. It was a bonus he had not expected. He knew he could not get a conviction on the evidence of the handkerchief alone, but he hoped to unnerve Andrew to the point where my cousin would make an open confession. And—aided by Anne's confession—he had succeeded.

About the espionage, Burgess had not been at all sure. But Charles had decided that it was Anne almost as soon as he heard about it. It was the only possible explanation, he had told Burgess, when he had gone in to see him the previous night. "It would be out of character for Andrew or Tay," Charles had insisted. "Murder, possibly; something like this, no. Uncle William's out of the question—so's his wife. So is Giles. So is Christy. So—though you may not believe it—am I. Anne is the logical, the only suspect. I haven't been an Intelligence Officer for nothing."

Burgess had been impressed but not completely convinced. He had not overlooked the possibility that Charles was seeking in this way to divert suspicion from himself. Anne's account of her interview early Saturday evening with Uncle Hugh had swayed Burgess somewhat towards Charles' theory. Then Giles had driven in the final nail.

Later that day, I spent some time explaining things as well as I could to the horrified staff, and trying to restore some semblance of domestic peace. I naturally did not tell them about Anne; but none of them had known that anything besides murder was involved. I tried to suggest that Andrew had been not quite normal lately, suffering from strain and overwork. I do not know how much of this they believed, but no one asked awkward or embarrassing questions. There seemed a tacit agreement to let the tragedy fade away as rapidly and as quietly as possible.

I told Mrs. Rapp that I should be staying on for a few days. "Mr. Charles will be here at least to-night, I think," I added. "I don't yet know what I'm going to do with the house. But in any case, I'll be pleased if you'd stay on to take care of it."

Mrs. Rapp looked pleased, but somewhat apprehensive. "I—it's not my business, really, Miss Christy, but—well, you wouldn't sell Feathers, would you? After all, you grew up here."

After all, I grew up there—and not only in the way she had meant. I hadn't consciously been aware of my intentions before, but I smiled at her. "No," I said. "I may not live here immediately, but I shan't sell Feathers."

When I went into the library, Charles looked up from something he was writing. He told me it was his resignation from the Foreign Office.

I had never thought of him as doing any other job or living any other way than as a diplomat, and I was very much surprised. "Surely they aren't as stuffy as all that to-day," I said. "I agree it's a bit embarrassing for them to have someone whose father's been murdered by his cousin. I don't suppose they'll learn about Anne. But it's not your fault. And people will forget it all as soon as there's a new sensation."

"Oh, I think they'd be all right about it," said Charles. "As you say, they might find it embarrassing at first, but they'd get over it. I'm not doing it for that reason. You see, I'm taking on a new job, Christy. I'm going to begin learning to run the business."

I could not believe he was serious. "But you've *never* been interested in the business. Why now?"

"That's not strictly true," said my cousin. "There were various reasons why I never considered going into it before. I wouldn't have worked with my father, for one thing. I was fond of him, but I learned when I was very young what he did to people who worked with him—in the business, that is. Your case was different. But running a large business like that is interesting—and anyway, someone's got to do it. A lot of people's money—mostly family money—is tied up in it."

"But Tay?"

"Yes. You know, Christy, I was right about Tay and Andrew. Andrew was a much tougher proposition altogether. If it had been the other way round—if Tay had murdered my father and been found out—Andrew wouldn't have turned a hair. He'd have congratulated himself on having been rid of a rival at no trouble to himself—and he'd have taken over the business. He'd probably have made much more money than I'm going to make for all of you, too. He had the enormous advantage of never being able to see anyone else's point of view—or even that anyone else had a point of view."

"You're probably right," I said. "But what about Tay?"

"Tay isn't so tough. He was sickened by what he was willing to do, himself, to get control. But when he saw what Andrew was willing to do, he couldn't take it. He just doesn't want anything to do with the business any more. He says he'll vote the shares he was left to control any way I want. He'll also give me advice, if I ask for it. But he literally doesn't want to go near the business again. Luckily, there are a couple of younger men who are very competent, he says. Anyway, that gives me control of 50 per cent of the voting stock. So unless you're planning to start an opposition party——"

We both smiled. The idea was so new to me that I was still having trouble assimilating it. But Charles was clearly quite serious.

"Do you think you'll like it?" I asked.

"Oh, yes. I think so. There are a lot of problems to be solved, and that's always interesting. Anyway, it won't be my entire life. Did you ever think, Chris, what those four men—my father, Tay, Andrew, and Giles—all had in common?"

"A love for power?"

"Well, yes, if you want to put it that way. But the sad and important fact is that they hadn't much *else* in their lives—much that meant anything, I mean. Tay never married. My father was married only very briefly. Giles isn't married. And Andrew's marriage, I've always thought, was more of a façade than a real and important thing to him—more like an institution than a personal relationship. Whether they wanted power because they didn't have anything else to care about, or whether they couldn't care about anything else because they wanted power, is a subject for discussion."

I laughed. "It doesn't matter."

"Well," said Charles, "the point is, I'm going to avoid that. My marriage is going to be very important to me, and so are my children.

And the business is going to occupy a reasonable, but not a disproportionate, place in my life."

"I suppose that depends to some extent on the girl you marry," I suggested. "Have you selected her yet?"

"Yes," said Charles. "As a matter of fact, I've had my eye on her for some time. She made a rather unwise marriage and got herself into a bit of a mess. But she seems to have pulled out of it now. And I'm sure it'll be a success—that is," he said, and his voice changed, "if she loves me as much as I love her."

I stared at the cousin I had known all my life.

It was as if one had suddenly found the key piece in a puzzle one had been working on for a long time. All the other pieces fell miraculously into place. When Charles said those words, the disjointed pieces of my life seemed suddenly to form a clear pattern. This was the end to which everything had been leading.

I had been leaning against his desk as he sat in the chair, looking at me. Our eyes met with complete understanding.

"She does," I said.

THE END